Laura Hawks

soaring on the wings
of the written word

DEDICATION

I would like to dedicate this book to my mother, who is always and forever in my heart. She was the encouragement I sometimes needed. She was the person who was proud of every accomplishment I had. She was my supporter in every part of my life and she was my best friend. She will always be missed.

I would also like to dedicate this book to my mother's sisters, the last of which passed May 2018. My mother was one of eight children and many had a strong influence on my life. I will miss the feeling of family they always instilled within me and the love and safety I was always surrounded by.

I hope all of you take the time to appreciate your parents, for they are everything in the universe.

GUMSHOE AND THE MYSTERIOUS MUSHROOM

ACKNOWLEDGMENTS

I wish to thank my friend Adrian, who has been so helpful in giving me the push I've needed to write. What she thought of as nagging was actually the encouragement to sit down and write, always excited to know about my next project and giving me her ear when I just needed someone to talk to.

Thank you to all of my fans. Each of your notes, emails and posts have been very much appreciated, especially during these past months darkened by so much loss.

After you finish reading this book, I hope you will also take the time to let me know your thoughts. Platforms to contact me are located in the back of the book under About The Author. I would also greatly appreciate it if you would leave a review on Amazon and/or Goodreads.

Thank you again for your patronage and friendship.

FURTHER BOOKS BY LAURA HAWKS:

Words For Warriors II: A Word Search Book
The Balconies of New Orleans

(Please note: The following are adult books)

Demon Trilogy: Demon's Kiss
                     Demon's Dream
                     Demon's Web

Spirit Walker's Thrillers:
                     Shifter's Hope
                     Shifter's Pride
                     Shifter's Journey

Ghost and the Grimoire

Fractured Fairytales:
                     Snow White & The 7 Cannibals

Valley View Mysteries:
                     Flaming Retribution

Chapter One

'*The circle of life. Take a breath, with each one bringing you closer to the end of life. Yours. Someone else's. The young take it for granted. Life that is. Death is the furthest thing from their minds. It certainly wasn't a part of my thoughts. At least, I don't remember it that way. Memories are mostly a void, a blackness in my mind, but I get the distinct impression of certain aspects. I feel my life was just beginning.*

'*I continue to watch the old, once young and full of energy, then middle aged and starting families of their own before meandering through life as the young play at their feet, unaware that in the blink of an eye they will be elderly and wondering where all the time went or how they got so mature so quickly so as not to recognize the wrinkled face and gray hairs reflected back to them in the mirror. I know my appearance is nothing like I remember...the youthful handsomeness no longer staring back at me.*

'*I remember I found a beautiful dame who still makes me smile at the thought of her, even if I can't remember her name. I married her, and she gave me a beautiful little girl. Who thought of the circle of life then? Of Death? Of the ages that have long passed and will continue to do so for all eternity? I certainly hadn't. Not then. The world was too perfect. A job I loved, a beginning family, nothing could be better.'*

He lifted his head up. The colorful sky beautiful; with blue, orange, red swirling among big, soft, white cotton-ball-looking clouds passing by serenely without a care in the world. Some of the billowy puffs made recognizable shapes before they slid into unrecognizable blobs as they moved across the sky.

Couples walked hand in hand along the shore of the lake or sat cuddled together. Children ran around their parents or ahead of their grandparents, while the latter meandered along the paved pathway enjoying the antics of the young. People walked their dogs, teenagers rollerbladed or used hoverboards to glide past those who were in no hurry to go anywhere.

The scene was serene, tranquil, but for him, sad. He thought the world was his oyster, his life just blossoming into a wonderful adventure with so much to experience and look forward to. What little he could remember of his life was experiencing a lot of death, mostly as a result of a war. It was *war* after all. But he returned home. Safe and whole. The woman he loved had waited for him and once he was back home in Illinois, he knew he couldn't let another day go by without making her his forever. Yet forever didn't last as long as he thought it would.

He focused his eyes on the young couple pushing a stroller while holding hands. His heart tightened in his chest. He missed his wife and the adorable, curly-blonde-haired baby girl that was the result of the love they had for each other. The sense of self rode through him. Surely, as he was now, he shouldn't be having these memories. Or shouldn't be facing the black hole of despair over what memories he'd lost. Everything was just beyond his grasp. Nothing tangible. Nothing real. Occasional wisps of his life as it once was flickered into being and just as quickly disappeared, slipping through his fingers into oblivion.

How cruel life could be. Ever changing, ever fluid. Time really didn't stand still, and time really didn't heal. It just allowed pain to become more bearable, but not always. There were still moments, like these, that caused him to cringe in the painful losses, caused him to forget how to even breathe as his chest would tighten so much it was a physical ache that, after all this time, was still unbearable. It brought his current situation to a prominent realization, even more forcefully once again, of how much things had been altered in his very existence.

Inwardly, he sighed. He missed his family terribly and, despite how little he remembered, he knew the heartache of their loss would never truly subside. Lifting his head, he turned back to the sunset and the colorful horizon. The circle of life blossomed all around him and increased his melancholy. He hated it. Detested the circumstances that brought him here today. He longed to know what happened to his family. Had they started anew after his human death? Had they forgotten him entirely? He wished he could remember them more. Their names, the sound of their voice, anything. However, it would also be nice if he remembered his own name and how he got here like this. Nothing made sense to him. Nothing seemed real.

He watched the setting sun, his furry tail twitching behind him.

Chapter Two

Adam Thomas, tall, distinguished; his dark brown hair and sharp blue eyes missed nothing as he moved around the bustling kitchen. It was like watching an ice skater move so fluidly. A twirl here, a spin there. A taste of a pot from this area, another from that. A few instructions to his prep staff as he pivoted about the floor. To the untrained eye, it'd be mind boggling with all the work going on simultaneously and yet so fluidly and effortlessly. The team of workers meshed as if one machine, each knowing what needed to be done.

Adam's chef jacket was splashed with various sauces and liquids, the only indication he was bustling about so quickly: pulling one pan out, checking on another, finger testing a third, then wiping his hands on his black jacket. He wore the black for prep, grey for front of house, and white later in the evening when it was starting to slow down. At least, that's how it was at the other restaurant he worked at before the Forbidden Fruit, and he hadn't planned on changing his routine.

The difference was Adam wasn't just the head chef at the Forbidden Fruit, he was also the owner, along with his wife, Evelyn. Evelyn had a degree in business management. It was how the two of them met nineteen years ago. In college. Evelyn was the quiet, leggy blonde with brown eyes who attended the school's culinary night. The student chefs were also the servers, and Adam waited on her. When the meal was over, they sat and talked until the custodians turned out the lights. He walked her back to her dorm that night, and they've been together ever since.

She supported him when he transferred to the Culinary Institute of America. He supported her when she decided to go for her master's degree in business, minoring in accounting. After a couple of years of dating, they married and, a year later, Evelyn gave birth to their daughter Amelia, Mia for short. It was Mia who actually named the new venture. Many called her mom Eve for short and Mia always teased them she was their forbidden fruit. Adam thought it the perfect name for his new restaurant.

Mia took after Adam and his love of cooking. Unlike her mother, Mia didn't really have a head for numbers, though she enjoyed some of the other aspects, like inventory and going through the applicants to hire. Regardless of all the business end Mia might have liked, her passion was to be in the kitchen cooking. She started alongside Adam at the age of three, learning how to cook. By age five, Mia had tested items of her own and was creating full-course meals. Adam helped to hone her skills and they both encouraged her in her passion to cook and bake.

Now, in the restaurant, he hired his daughter as a prep cook, but unlike the others he hired for that same position, he gave his almost-fifteen-year-old daughter a bit more leeway. At home the two would discuss menus and what she'd contribute to the dinners. Of course, she only got to work as long as her grades were good, and she emphatically promised to maintain her studies.

Tonight was the opening night of the Forbidden Fruit and, although she had school, Mia was allowed to miss this one Friday in order to get everything ready for service. Mia proudly planned one full course. A five-mushroom soup, a cranberry-orange arugula salad, pan-seared duck breast with a blood orange glaze, citrus-and-bacon-roasted Brussels sprouts, twice-baked sweet potato with caramelized pecans, and a chocolate crème Brule for dessert. There was a lot to do, but Adam knew his daughter could handle it.

As head chef, Adam tasted every dish, for it had to be perfect, tonight more than any other. Evelyn was working on the front of house, dealing with the servers, the linens, and the final touches of décor. Everything had to be perfect. They were sold out, reservation wise, including having a table of food critics that they all knew could make or break their fledging enterprise.

Adam moved over to Henry's work station, watching him clean the fish. Henry looked up, suddenly nervous over the scrutiny. His hands shaking, Henry accidently sliced his hand as he fileted a whitefish.

Adam grumbled, moving to the first aid kit. "You're the third person tonight to cut themselves. Seems to be an epidemic of nerves and I'm the one with the opening night."

"We all just want everything perfect for you. We know how important tonight is."

"Then all of you need to work without injury and more carefully. There are a lot of bones left and I don't need a customer getting one stuck in their throat."

"Yes, Chef."

"Have Dominic check your fish before cooking."

"Yes, Chef."

"And watch your knife. Cut the fish, not yourself." Adam put the kit away. Maybe he was making everyone jumpy with his micromanaging, but this was his first venture as a business owner and therefore he was even more insistent on everything being perfect.

Arriving at his sous chef's station, Adam leaned in to talk softly. "Dominic, keep an eye on the fish. Henry is still leaving bones in and I don't need anyone choking on some small fish bone. Check his work before he cooks. I told him he is to check with you before he puts it in the pan."

"You got it, Chef. I'll check on his progress as soon as I finish up here." Dominic held the knife down while speaking, turning away from the rack of lamb he was prepping.

"Have you had a chance to taste the sauces yet from Lee's station?"

"I have. I told him the Bruere Blanc was a bit salty and the Béarnaise was a bit too thick."

Adam nodded. "Good. I told him the same thing and gave him suggestions on how to correct them." True, Adam could've just fixed them himself, but he wanted his team to know how to deal with problems on their own and for the future. "I'll be checking on them again to make sure he corrected them. Good job, Dominic."

Dominic nodded and returned to butchering the

lamb for prep. "Mia's doing good, though."

"Don't be buttering me up just because she's my daughter. Here she's an employee and will be held to the same standards I expect from everyone. Even myself." Adam patted Dominic on the shoulder. He knew he had to make sure the other cooks didn't feel like they were being held to a different level from his own daughter. He wanted everyone to feel equal, despite the different titles they had.

Adam looked around his kitchen, proud that, although this was the first time they were really altogether, they worked like a well-oiled machine. Finally, he turned to his daughter's station. She was moving about rapidly, stirring two pots at a time, chopping her vegetables, juicing her fruit. Adam couldn't have been prouder watching his teenage daughter.

Although Adam would admit to being a bit prejudice, he knew it couldn't appear that way to his other employees. With a purposeful stride, he walked over to Mia's station, clean spoon in hand to test the sauces and dressings she was making. He breathed in the scent of the sauce, then tasted. New spoon and repeated the procedure with the soup. Watched as she prepped the duck breast, slicing the skin for a better and crispier cook. She was still chopping the mushrooms, and the blood orange were being juiced for the duck sauce. She also had on a pan to crisp up the bacon with the Brussels sprouts. "The soup is a bit loose."

"I know, Dad, I mean, Chef. I'm going to add some heavy cream to thicken once I get it to the flavor I like. It's not quite there yet, but I'm not sure why."

"What does your palate say?"

Mia smiled. Her dad knew she had a good palate and trusted her senses with regards to spices and flavors. "It's missing something. I'm thinking maybe a touch of garlic?"

Adam used another spoon to taste the soup again. "It's a bit earthy right now, so maybe if you roast the garlic first, it might provide the flavor you were hoping for?"

"Ah. I should've thought of roasted garlic first. Great idea." Turning, she left her workstation to head into the kitchen, grabbing several cloves of garlic. They roasted better in their own skins, so she didn't bother chopping them up. She'd do that when they were ready to be added to the soup. Sticking the pan of garlic cloves in the oven, she turned her attention back to her dad, who was still there.

"Is something else off?"

"I'm not sure. Probably not."

"What are you thinking?" Mia was perplexed, looking around her station and wondering if she'd forgotten anything, even though she had her menu notes on the small stand of her work area.

"Just the mushroom soup. It's off, but I can't place as to why. Might just be the lack of garlic or something else. Call me when you've added the garlic and given it time to infuse its flavor."

"Are you thinking if I can't get it right, we'll 86 it?" She didn't want to pull an item from the menu, much less one she was in charge of, but if it wasn't 100% perfect, she knew he'd cancel it.

"Let's see first. I don't want to 86 anything this early in the game. We've got a couple of hours to fix it. It might just be the mix of mushrooms. All that earthiness is overwhelming the broth."

"Yeah. Maybe cream will smooth it out better, so it'll still be rich but not quite so earthy."

"You're doing a great job, Poppy. Don't worry about it." Adam used his nickname for his daughter, knowing it'd ease her concerns.

"Hey! Where is the big man?" A deep, rich voice bellowed. Turning, Adam and Mia both recognized Earl Dapper, owner of Rocks Bar and Grill.

Adam smiled as he walked over to shake Earl's hand. "What are you doing here?"

"Came to wish you a successful opening night. Still hate losing you as my head chef and taking Dominic with you, but the restaurant looks good."

"Thanks, Earl. I heard you moved Jeremy up to head chef. He did well under me, I know he'll do a great job for you too."

"He ain't got your presence. I think he thinks he's still on the line and forgets to call out the orders."

"He'll grow into it. I know he will, and his food is good."

"He will. So, you ready for tonight?"

"Almost. A few more things to prep, and then ready to have the guests come in."

"Nervous?" Earl looked around the kitchen with the eye of a long-time restauranteur.

"Not really. More excited and anxious then nervous."

"You've worked for someone else for quite a number of years. Running your own place is much different."

"I know. But I like having more control over my menus, and Eve is great for the books and management, so I can still focus on what I love."

"Well, I'll be back tonight. I just wanted to wish you good luck and get a glimpse of the place before you got too hectic."

"Thanks for stopping by." He shook hands with Earl again, walking him towards the back door.

When the door opened, Mia saw a beautiful Siamese cat peering in. Like her mom, Mia loved animals and she worried this one was probably hungry and looking for food. Scooping up a bit of her duck scraps, she seared them quickly, then headed out to feed the poor little thing. She didn't see the feline at first, but called to him to see if he was nearby. He might have smelled the food, or he heard her, but soon he peeked his head out from behind the dumpster. She had the scraps of duck on a small plate. "It's okay little guy. We'll have lots of food for you. This is just for starts." She set the plate down and stepped back. "Hmm, no collar," she mused. "Hope the animal catcher doesn't get you." She re-entered the business and got back to her work after she washed her hands.

Chapter Three

The restaurant was hopping. So many came, they quickly turned over tables three and four times before the night settled down. Adam and Eve were ecstatic. Things were going well, and if it stayed like this, they were going to have a success on their hands. People had always liked Adam's food. They would frequently find out where he was or what nights he was working just to have him as their chef. They knew no matter what they ordered, it'd be prepared perfectly. Adam was a stickler for not letting anything leave his kitchen unless he okayed it. He had a reputation for getting clean plates and having very few returned with any issues. His opening night was no disappointment.

Halfway through service, Mia had to 86 the mushroom soup. Not because she hadn't fixed the issue from earlier, but because they ran out. They ran out of a lot of things throughout service, not anticipating that people would order two or three of everything early on. By the end of the night, they had very little left and the entire staff was exhausted.

Mia took out a couple of bags of garbage from her station and those nearby. She noticed the duck scraps were gone, so brought the plate back in. On another trip, she noticed the Siamese was still nearby, so brought out some of the fish scraps, checking quickly to make sure there were no bones. Leaving the plate out again, she returned to cleaning up. She couldn't remember being so tired.

She'd had a few opportunities to go into the restaurant itself, whether it was Eve or Adam who wanted to show her off or for people who just wanted to meet the person who made one of her menu items. She recognized many who visited. Mr. and Mrs. Hennessy, whose cow was infamously being tipped over. Mrs. and Mr. Antonio, her history teacher and her husband. The Chase family, of which she was friends with their son Caleb. Police detective and friend of the family, Phil Hardy. Police Chief Decker and his family. The Summer family, whose roots went as far back as the founder of the town, James Summer. (The Summer Statue in the town square was infamous for being vandalized yearly in a pink tutu and red paint for lipstick and rouge when the school season was over. It happened like clockwork, but only the city's officials seemed to mind, and then mostly because of the money it cost to clean it up.)

In a small town, such as the Midlands, it was easy

to know most everyone, and as such, hard to keep any secrets. Yet, Mia couldn't think of any place she'd rather be. She loved the town and its strange, sometimes oddball people. The Midlands was the perfect place. It had its own lake, Lake Henderson, perfect for boating, fishing and swimming. It was close enough to the bigger town of Plainview and only forty-five minutes to Bloomington/Normal, which was probably where she'd go to college when the time was right.

Before she knew it, the last customer was leaving and she could finally collapse. Mia checked on the plate she'd left for the cat. Seeing it empty once again, she brought the plate in and added it to the dishwasher's pile. Her station cleaned, she took the last of the trash out and was about to meet her mom to head home when the phone rang.

Eve answered and spoke for a few minutes in hushed tones. Mia wondered what that was about, but didn't give it much thought until it rang again almost immediately upon disconnecting from the first call. Again, Mia couldn't totally hear what was being said on the other line, but from the look on her face, Eve wasn't too happy with the conversation. When she hung up the phone this time, she called to her husband. "Adam!"

Poking his head out of the kitchen, Adam instinctively knew whatever his wife needed, it wasn't something to be yelled through the now-empty-of-customers restaurant. Mia quickly joined the two of them so she'd know what was going on as well. Before Eve could speak, the phone rang again and Eve answered, jotting down their names on a pad of paper nearby.

"We've got a problem. Seems something in our food is making people sick."

Adam scowled. "What do you mean? Sick, how?"

"I've gotten three phone calls so far about people being nauseous and not feeling well. Almost like they have the stomach flu, but since this was the last place they ate, and the symptoms started coming over them the last few hours, they thought we should know about it. They're concerned it might be food poisoning."

"I checked everything myself. Unless I didn't catch a cross-contamination somewhere that someone did… Shit. I don't know. Did you get all their info?"

"Yes. I'll look online for forms we can use. I didn't think I would need them this quickly. I also jotted down what they had to see if we can find a common denominator as to what they all ate. I'll also check the book to see if they were here about the same time and where I had them seated. Might be someone was sick they sat near and it was contagious."

"I'll check my kitchen for any cross-contamination. I know the food was all fresh. I bought most of it at the farmers' market this morning. However, let's talk to Phil and have him keep an ear out for anyone having gotten sick. It might be something in the vegetables that would be undetected to us and remained even after washing. Or you could be correct and it's the flu actually going around and possibly spread to other patrons while they were here."

"Hopefully, it will just be the three people, but we'll need to investigate to make sure we're not at fault, and if we are, then we'll need to contact our insurance company and handle it through them to make sure everyone is taken care of. I really don't need this kind of shit on opening night. It was going so well." Eve twisted her hair to put into a loose ponytail. "I'm sure you took every precaution possible. Finish up, investigate. I'm going to take Mia home and get Maddie from Mrs. Saunderson. I'll bring the books home and go through them when I get a chance tonight."

Maddie, short for Madison, was Mia's four-year-old

sister who had a proclivity to always wear a cape, golden belt, wrist bracelets, and the tiara of Wonder Woman, who loved to dash about trying to save everyone in her invisible plane or use her gold-colored cord to make her family tell the truth.

Adam kissed Eve and patted Mia on the head. "You did good today, Poppy. Get some rest. I'll see you both at home later." Turning, he headed into the kitchen to see he if could figure out what happened to make some people sick.

Chapter Four

Mia had been anxious all day. Her nerves were taut and waiting for a culmination of some event. She'd always had a sense when major things were about to occur. Her bestie, Zoe Fuller, calls her cray-cray whenever Mia confides in her about her feelings. Zoe would then joke and say Mia's Spidey senses were going haywire again.

Lately, Mia had kept her foreboding senses to herself. She didn't want to be made fun of. As it were, she was not the popular girl in class. She didn't consider herself very pretty. She got the brown hair of her dad and hazel eyes that she assumed were a mixture of her dad's blue ones and her mom's brown ones. The girls she hung out with, which included Zoe, weren't the popular girls. They weren't nerdy either. They just were. Nothing special, nothing important, mostly invisible. Usually, Mia was okay with that. She didn't want to spend time being the cheerleader, or sitting around playing chess games, or debating in the debate club. She wanted to cook. That was her passion.

Today was her birthday. She felt she should be planning her fifteenth birthday party. But too many were still ill or just recovering and the restaurant had taken a hit since opening a week ago, with much of the clientele dropping off, including the families of her friends. Some students were back today for the first time, others were still recouping. Yet the events of opening night and all the illnesses that had been reported didn't seem to be the cause for her jumpiness. Besides, fifteen wasn't that big of a deal unless you were Hispanic and having a Quinceanera celebration, like her friend Tiffany. For the rest of her class, it was Sweet Sixteen parties that were the big blowouts of their teenage years. Maybe it was because everyone seemed to forget it was her birthday and it bothered her. She expected her friends, especially Zoe, to have remembered.

Mia's eyes went to the clock on the wall. She'd lost track of Mrs. Antonio's lecture on the War of 1812. Although she's one of the better instructors telling the stories of the past as if she'd actually lived them, today Mia just couldn't focus on the lessons. Her head was spinning in a thousand directions, mostly with regards to the Forbidden Fruit, but they also drifted to uncovering what could've made so many ill. Her father and her spent hours in the days after in an attempt to find a reliable source of contamination. It just didn't make sense. She also thought about the cat she'd been feeding the past week in the back of the restaurant. It seemed to be waiting for her to bring him some food and grateful when she fed him. He still didn't get close to her, but she was okay with that. As long as she knew it wasn't starving and assumed it was doing okay otherwise, she was content. Her mother said it was probably feral, which was why it wouldn't come close to her. If Eve had her way, she'd bring the creature home and find it a new family. That was the kind of person Eve was. She had a huge heart, especially when it came to animals or children, and she could be fierce when either one needed protection from harm.

Mia raised her eyes again to the wall timekeeper. The ticking seemed to be mocking her, even though she knew how absurd the prospect was. Zoe tapped her fingers on the desk almost in time with slowly passing seconds. *They say a watched pot never boils.* The thought seemed random in her head, but at the moment appeared very true.

Mia turned back to Mrs. Antonio, attempting to concentrate on the lesson, but it didn't work. Her mind continued to drift. She should be doing something, not listening to what already happened so long ago. When the bell rang, its echoing loudness caused Mia to jump. She'd been so lost in her own thoughts about what she could do to help uncover the truth behind the illnesses, the booming sound startled her. Scooping up her books, Zoe joined her as she made a dash for the door.

"Amelia?" Mrs. Antonio called, causing Mia to stop and turn to face her teacher.

"Yes?"

Zoe whispered, "I'll meet you outside."

"Please inform your mother I'll see you both tonight after the sun goes down."

Mia became nervous. "Am I in trouble?"

Mrs. Antonio shook her head once, almost sternly. "No." After a brief pause, she added, "Your mother asked to see me. Didn't she talk to you about it?"

Somehow, that didn't make Mia feel any better, but she shook her head. "No, she didn't. I'll relay the message."

Mrs. Antonio gave her a curt nod before dismissing her. She watched Mia hastily depart the room. Donna wasn't pleased Eve hadn't prepared her daughter for what was about to come. Time was running out, and if Eve didn't educate the fifteen-year-old on how her life was about to drastically change, she might have to take matters into her own hands.

As promised, Zoe was waiting outside the room for her and together they walked towards their lockers. Her squad, made up of Cathy, Karen, Shania, Lynda and Tiffany, were waiting in the hall by her locker.

"What's going on?" Mia asked. True, the group of girls got together often, but rarely meeting by a locker.

The girls moved aside so Mia could see the decorations covering her cubicle. Shania stepped from the back of the group and held out a container of cupcakes. Mia burst into a smile. Her friends remembered after all.

"You thought we forgot, didn't you?" Zoe smirked.

"It crossed my mind." Stowing her books quickly, Mia led them out to the school lawn.

"We'd never do that." Lynda side bumped her.

"We knew you were busy with your dad's restaurant and all, so we waited." Shania passed out a cupcake to each of them.

"Plus, I wasn't sure if I was going to be coming back to school today or not. I'm still feeling a bit off," Cathy admitted.

They all took out their phones and put the candle app on it. Mia laughed as they sang "Happy Birthday," then she blew out the candle apps.

"What time do you have to be at work today?" Karen pulled the wrapper away from the dark chocolate cake with white icing and multicolored sprinkles.

"I'm only stopping in for a few minutes. As long as I'm there before 4:30, I'll be good. Mom wants to bring me home early. I thought it was for a party or something, but Mrs. Antonio is coming over, so I'm not sure what it's all about."

Each of the girls handed her a small, wrapped gift. Cathy gave her a necklace with a butcher knife on it. Karen gave her some nail polish. Shania got her a gift card for Monroe's Department Store, a local place in town. Lynda had wrapped a USB flash drive; "It has 150 songs on it and there is room for more to add." Zoe handed her a box containing a pillow with glitter on it that read "Follow Your Dreams."

Thanking each of the girls in turn, she realized she should head to the restaurant before she got into trouble.

"You're still going to meet us tomorrow for the finishing up of our posters, right?" Zoe popped the last of her cupcake into her mouth, her cheeks bulging with the confection.

"My poster is mostly done, but I'll put the final

touches on it at the library tomorrow as planned."

They all walked over to the bike racks, unlocking their bicycles and heading in different directions, with Mia heading down the main road towards the center of town.

As she neared the restaurant, she was astonished to find a couple of squad cars parked nearby, some with their lights flashing. Her heart raced with concern and she pedaled faster. Hopping off her bike, she had to wade through a couple of rows of people to get to the front of the line. She could hear folks whispering as she tried to get by, but their words made no sense.

A tall officer, dressed in Midlands blues, moved to block her path. "Sorry, you can't go any further."

"I work there. My parents own the place. What's going on?" Although she was talking to the officer, her eyes were darting behind him, trying desperately to see what was happening. Then she spotted Phil and her dad coming out the front door. "Dad! Detective Hardy!" Mia called to them, waving to get their attention.

Phil said something to Adam, then moved towards Mia. "It's okay, Kevin. Let her through."

Kevin stepped aside to let Mia pass before returning to his previous stance of making sure no one else entered the area.

Propping her bicycle against the building, she ran to her dad, hugging him. "What's going on? What's happening?"

"It's going to be okay, Poppy."

"I don't understand. Dad? Phil?"

Phil rubbed the back of his neck. "Mia, I'm taking your dad in for questioning."

"Why?"

"Because, the Hennessys died. Both of them from something they ate here."

"No. It's been a week since the Hennessys were here. They came opening night only."

"Yes, and they've been sick. We thought it was the stomach flu or food poisoning, but then they started to get better. It turns out, though they were feeling better, their organs were decaying."

"They're in their 70s, of course their organs were decaying. They were old." Twirling her hair, a habit Mia did when she was upset or nervous, her voice rose in her current state.

"They were decaying because of poisonous mushrooms. The CDC classified the culprit."

"We don't serve poisonous mushrooms. We got all

ours from the farmers' market that morning. I was with Dad when he picked them out."

"That's why we are only taking your dad in for questioning and he's not under arrest yet. He'll be home in time for dinner."

"This just doesn't make sense. Dad, have him go talk to Mr. Meyers, where we bought the mushrooms. He'll tell you. He didn't sell us poisonous ones. He couldn't. It's against the law."

Adam stepped forward. Thankfully, he wasn't humiliated by being handcuffed. "I already did. Mr. Meyers is currently missing. When they find him, they'll talk to him too. It'll be okay. Go on inside and meet your mom. I'll see you in a little bit." Adam kissed her forehead and headed towards Phil's car. Before Phil followed him, he turned to Mia. "I know this is kind of shitty, but I'm going to do everything I can. You know he's my friend too. I won't make it to your house later, but I did want you to have this. Happy birthday." He handed her a long thin box, then moved to speak to the other officers still there.

Mia held the gift in her hand, watching until Phil and her dad drove away. One of the other squads also left, but one remained behind, pulling to parallel park and turning off his lights. Mia ignored him and entered the restaurant. It was dark and quiet, giving her a foreboding feeling that tingled down to her toes. She heard some voices coming from the kitchen, where she could also see light from around the door frame.

She slipped the gift into her backpack and entered the kitchen. Dominic and Eve were talking; Lee, Henry and the other cooks were standing around together, whispering quietly. All conversation stopped when she entered the room, making her feel very self-conscious. She headed over to stand by her mom, but Eve suggested she wait outside for a bit.

Unsure of what else to do, Mia grabbed some tuna fish and a plate and headed out to the back. She set the plate down, then moved across the alleyway to sit on the stoop of the opposite building.

"Poisonous mushrooms?" Mia talked to herself in disbelief. "I made the soup. I cut up the mushrooms and put them in the soup. Somehow this is my fault. I served them. What have I done?"

"You didn't do anything. You didn't pick them out, so this isn't your fault."

The voice rang in her head, her ears heard faint meows. She looked up and around, trying to see who was talking to her. The only thing she saw was the Siamese cat she'd been feeding the past week. She shook her head to clear it of cobwebs she was sure were there.

She watched the feline move towards the food she'd left for him. He sniffed it, but then skirted around it to go behind the dumpster. *Odd,* she thought at his bypassing the food.

She watched the cat move around, almost searching for something, though she couldn't imagine what. "Meow. Meow. Mew. Meep. Eep. Meoooow." The Siamese sat regally on top of the dumpster, staring at her.

However, she heard something more than just the sounds made from a feline creature. *Wonderful. I turn fifteen and I get to go bonkers. I swear I heard him in my head and it actually made sense. I'm hallucinating, or so lit I've lost it.*

"Darn it. I forgot you can't understand me." The cat seemed to grumble and jump off the dumpster, wandering down the alleyway.

Mia rubbed her forehead. "This just can't be possible. Cats don't speak English."

The Siamese stopped and stared at her. "Meow, meep?"

Mia heard, *"Do you understand me, kitten?"*

She gasped, standing quickly and taking a step back only to trip on the stoop and fall back down on her rump. The cat moved cautiously closer to her. "Mew?" {*How?*}

Mia shrugged in answer to the question, but covered her mouth to stop herself from screaming at the same time. She had no clue what was going on, but if she wasn't totally crazy, she was understanding what this cat said to her. *Great. Now I'm Doctor Doolittle,* she thought to herself. "Zoe's right. I've gone off the deep end and am Cray-Cray with a capital C."

The Siamese tilted his head, watching her with large, blue, unblinking eyes. "Meow, meow, mew, mew, meow, mew." {*If you really understand me, look behind the dumpster.*}

"I'm insane. I'm really in looneyland. I'm talking to myself and being answered by a cat that I can understand. This is so wrong on so many levels." Breathlessly, cautiously, Mia stood and skirted around the small cat as if he would attack, even though part of her was sure he wouldn't. She didn't know why she was following his instructions, she just knew she had to. Using all the strength she had, she pulled the heavy dumpster away from the brick wall to look behind it. On the ground was a partially bloodied glove. At first she didn't know why it mattered, but then she noticed there was something rotting and mushy on the outside. Whatever it was seemed stuck on the plastic glove, and they had handled it after they had cut themselves. Could it be the remnants of a mushroom? Mia was sure she was the only one who handled the mushrooms after they got back from the farmers' market. Then she remembered she had Henry clean and dry them.

She went inside and called for the remaining officer who was standing in the kitchen like some sentinel. Grudgingly, he followed her after he told the rest to remain where they were. Once outside, Kevin looked around. "What'd'ya want to show me?"

"Behind the dumpster. I'm not sure if it's anything, but to me it looks like one of our gloves with a touch of blood inside and what looks like a rotten mushroom outside. I thought it might be evidence."

Giving her a doubting look, he peered behind the heavy metal container and spotted what she was referring to. "Did you touch it?"

"No."

"Don't. I'll get an evidence bag from the car and be

right back." He quickly hastened down the alleyway towards the street.

Mia turned to the cat and stared. She felt like she was going insane. Or maybe she just imagined it all. Moments later, Officer Easton returned with a plastic bag marked evidence in bright red letters across it. Using the inside of the bag, he picked up the discarded glove, turned the bag back and sealed it. "Good work," he mumbled, then headed back into the kitchen.

The cat moved over to sit beside Mia. Without a word, she stared at him in confusion.

"Meow, meow?" {*You can really hear me?*}

"Yes. I don't know how, but I can. How can you even be talking to me so that I understand what you're saying? I'm dreaming, right? I've turned fifteen and am now having a nervous breakdown. Or those cupcakes got me lit on something higher than chocolate."

Eve walked out then. "Mia? Who are you talking to?" The older woman moved to sit next to her daughter.

"No one, Mom. Just flipping my lid is all."

"What do you mean? And who is your cute little friend?"

Mia shrugged. "I don't know. He's been coming around since opening night and I have been giving him some scraps of food." She didn't want to tell her mom why she suddenly felt the need to see a shrink and get some happy pills. Maybe she was on some TV show, like *Punk'd* or *Impractical Jokers*, and wondered when the hidden cameras were going to pop up.

"Were you talking to him?"

Mia gave her a puzzled look. "Sure. Why not? I was talking to the cat."

Eve tilted her head slightly as she looked the animal over. "And is he talking to you?"

"What?"

"Is the cat talking to you?" Eve was dead serious, but Mia felt like she entered the Twilight Zone. What was going on? Why would her mom even ask her something so bizarre?

Unsure, Mia didn't say anything. Maybe this was all a trap or a trick. She honestly didn't know what to think, so staying mute seemed the appropriate thing to do.

"What's his name?"

"I don't know. He doesn't have a collar."

"Ask him."

"What?" Mia was incredulous at the suggestion.

"Ask him what his name is. I'm sure he'll tell you."

Mia wasn't sure about the suggestion, but she turned to the cat. She didn't have anything to lose. "Okay, cat. What's your name?"

"Meow, meeew."

"What'd he say?"

Mia turned to her mother. "You're kidding, right?"

Eve shook her head. "I have a few things to tell you, but I need you to answer me first. If you are talking to him, I wonder if he isn't talking to you. And if he is, then, that's fantastic."

Still unsure, and feeling like it was all a colossal prank, Mia lowered her head. "He says he can't remember his name, but he likes being called Gumshoe."

Relief seemed to flow from Eve and she wrapped an arm around her daughter, pulling her in for a side hug. "Nice to meet you, Gumshoe. Welcome to the family. I think it's time the three of us head home. Mia, you and I have a lot to discuss, and I'm sure Gumshoe has a few questions of his own."

Without another word, Eve stood and led the way out of the alley, making sure the other two were following her.

Chapter Five

As Eve pulled up in the family's driveway, Mia spotted Mrs. Antonio on the porch. She'd forgotten with everything going on to tell her mother Mrs. Antonio's message about seeing her tonight. Guess it was pretty obvious Mrs. Antonio was coming over, and she brought friends: Ms. Kelly Lucas, the town's librarian, and another woman Mia was unfamiliar with but sure she'd seen about town on occasion.

Eve's face seemed to light up when she saw the three women waiting for them. Hurrying out of the vehicle, she rushed onto the porch to greet the waiting women. "Sorry if we're late. Adam was taken in by Detective Hardy for questioning on those who've been ill." Eve didn't want to admit the Hennessys died as a result. She was still processing that news herself.

"I heard the CDC is involved and says it's some kind of poisoning? Do you know what happened?" Donna held her stuffed sock monkey in her arms. Mia noticed the stuffed animal in the corner of the classroom, but she hadn't been aware Mrs. Antonio took it with her when class was completed. Donna was the tallest of the women, standing at an even six feet. Her short red hair blazed with the setting sun, but her brown eyes seemed to hide many secrets, yet were full of wisdom.

"Yes. The CDC are the ones who realized it's not airborne or anything, that it was something they ate. When the Hennessys died, they did an autopsy and learned it was death cap mushrooms. We're just not sure how they got into our restaurant, or where else they might've gotten them. If it were just them, it'd be another story entirely, but since others are suffering the effects, we just don't know what happened. All of our produce came from the farmers' market. I'm pretty positive Sam wouldn't sell death caps to anyone, much less Adam. Let's go inside."

"What about the little one?" Kelly looked around as she waited for Eve to open the door. She was the proverbial librarian, with mousy brown hair and wire-rim glasses. She had a good complexion that she seemed to hide behind the large glasses and mussed ponytail hairstyle. Kelly was more interested in her tomes than in looks. When she realized the town didn't have a great library, much less an adequate one, Kelly used her parents' inheritance and took it upon herself to open one of the best facilities in the county.

"Mrs. Saunderson has her until I call. She's aware

there's a lot going on and I'd need some time before I could pick up Maddie."

"Good, good," the unknown woman said, then looked Mia up and down, as if examining a fish on a hook. Her long silver hair blew about her face and she was constantly pushing it away.

"Mia, that's Mrs. Marion Drumsky." Eve swung the door wide, letting everyone else pile into the foyer before heading into the dining room. "She runs the pharmacy at Maxwell's, which is great for us when we need unique ingredients."

Mia walked in, followed by Gumshoe and the other ladies. Eve's last sentence didn't make any sense to her, but she let it go. There were times adults never made much sense. Mia debated if she should stay, but Marion answered her hesitation before she could consider it further. "So, you're fifteen today?"

"Yes."

"What time were you born?" Kelly asked, pulling out her pocket watch from her dress pocket to check the time against Mia's answer.

"2:18." Mia gave Eve a quizzical look at the women's odd queries.

Donna held up the small bag she was carrying in

her free hand. "Eve, we need glasses."

Eve took the bag and saw the bottle of wine. Bringing it over to a cupboard, she grabbed four glasses and poured some out in each glass.

Gumshoe hopped onto the table and stuck his nose in the air, getting a nice whiff of the alcohol. "Meeweep?" He used his nose against one of the glasses to make his point. The fact anyone actually understood him unsettled his already shaken nerves. Although he would've preferred bourbon, anything with a kick would be appreciated.

"And who is your friend?" Donna sat down on the recliner and crossed her legs, setting the sock monkey on the armrest as she nodded to the Siamese.

"Gumshoe," Mia responded.

"Have you told her yet? She didn't seem to know we were even coming over tonight when I talked to her in school, or have a clue as to what this night means for her." Donna turned to Eve.

"Oh, yeah. Mom? Mrs. Antonio said she'd see us tonight." Better late than never.

Eve rolled her eyes at her daughter, then shook her head. "No. I've not had the time or opportunity."

"Tell me what?" Mia determined this conversation

was about her, so she sat down.

"Meowww." Gumshoe moved to sit on the floor next to Mia. Eve brought him a small glass of wine, to which he quickly, and gratefully, lapped up with a slight slurping sound.

Mia gave her head a shake in disbelief, then turned her attention back to the other women.

"She found Gumshoe today," Eve informed the women, to which they seemed both surprised and in awe.

"I told you she'd be strong. Powerful," Marion stated proudly.

"I told you that," Donna stated, giving Marion a crooked smirk. "You need to tell her, Eve. I'm sure from the look on her face, she has many questions."

"I will." Eve stood, pacing slightly.

"What's going on? What's this got to do with Gumshoe? Or me?" Mia was getting anxious.

"Fine. Mia, you're a witch and Gumshoe's your familiar." Donna turned to Eve. "You took too long."

Eve sighed. "I was planning on easing her into it, not blurting it out." She turned to her daughter. "Mia, it's true. I'm a witch, as is Donna, Marion and Kelly. The four of us make up our coven. We're born into this, and at age fifteen we gain our powers. The first is finding our familiar, the one animal that we can hear, that speaks to us. Mine is Mystic, as you probably already guessed." Mystic was a raven freakishly close to Eve for as long as Mia could remember. She'd always thought the bird had just been a pet of her mom, but the closeness the two shared made sense if what the women told her was true.

Now Mia was intrigued. She knew a little bit about witches, but just the popular stuff, like on *Charmed*, or the stuff from the history books, like the witches of Salem. But to assume her mother was one, and her teacher and now herself, was just a bit mind boggling, even if it did answer a lot of questions. "Will Mystic talk to me now as well?"

"No. He'll only talk to me, as he's my familiar. Donna's is a Capuchin monkey named Minion. Kelly's is an owl called Athena, and Marion has a yellow rat snake named Milo. Our familiars are our responsibility and they take care of us on our journey."

"When did you and Gumshoe meet?" Donna inquired.

"I told you today." Eve gave Donna a look.

Mia shook her head. "Actually, I met him a week

ago at our opening. I've been feeding him daily, but today is the first day I heard him talk to me."

Donna nodded as she steepled her fingers against her lips. "Makes sense. Although finding one's familiar usually takes a couple of weeks. It's amazing you found each other so quickly. But then, the familiar always finds you. He chooses you to be his companion. You don't choose him. As for him talking to you today only, your linkage wouldn't have clicked in until you formally turned fifteen at 2:18."

"So, he knew I was a witch? That he was going to be my companion?"

"No. Most likely he was drawn to you but didn't know why. When he saw you and realized you could hear him, then he made the choice to remain by your side, just as he's doing now." Donna watched as Mia reached down and rubbed Gumshoe's head, hearing him purr.

Gumshoe again headed over to the open bottle and sat beside it. "Meowww. Mew. Meeeow?"

"What does he want?" Eve asked her daughter, who placed her hands in her lap when Gumshoe walked away.

"He wants to know if we've got anything stronger

than wine, and if so can he have some. Or a cigarette. Or both."

Eve raised her eyebrow as she faced Gumshoe directly. "There's technically no smoking in this house and no drinking either. I gave you a glass because this was a special circumstance. She's fifteen. You don't need to be showing her what not to do." Before turning back to the other women, she moved the now-empty glass out of reach.

"If she's already found her familiar, I wonder how quickly her other powers will form." Kelly pulled her glass from the table, taking a sip before holding it on her lap and away from Gumshoe, just in case he had any ideas of drinking from her cup now that his empty one had been removed.

"Powers? I get powers?" She wondered what she'd be able to do. Maybe Maddie had it correct and they were Wonder Women, able to do lots of powerful things. "What kind of things will I be able to do? Can I conjure up money when I need it? Or glamor so others think I'm older? What about turn invisible?"

Eve shook her head. "Your powers need to be used for good. Not personal gain. Not to bring harm to others. The consequences could be more severe than you realize."

"I'll teach you about potions. Those are my specialty." Marion pulled out a leather-bound journal. "This is for you to write your spells and potions down." Now the comment of access to unique items made much more sense than earlier. "Like your mother said, potions, like spells, can't be used for personal gain."

"What about if I want to cure my friend's common cold?" Mia was losing some of her excitement at having powers.

"It would depend on why, but off-hand I'd say no. You'd still be doing it for a personal gain, even if it is to make a friend or relative feel better. Every action will have a reaction. Every spell and potion will have a consequence. It all depends on how much you go against what is natural and how it will affect you that will determine on what the universe will extract as payment." Marion folded her hands in her lap. She once had the same questions, so understood how disappointing it must be for Mia to learn there were conditions to using her new abilities.

"Then what good are having powers, spells and potions?"

Eve crossed her legs, glancing at the clock. She still

had to pick up Maddie. "Mia. We are a coven in a society that doesn't believe in witches and has little tolerance for those who are different. Although things have changed immensely over the past decade or two, we still keep our abilities to a minimum. There are a multitude of solutions that can be obtained without the use of what we can do. Ours are for emergencies and to protect against the evil forces brought about by black covens or by nature itself. You'll learn all of this as time progresses. You're just learning everything now. Give us time to teach you everything you'll need to defend yourself from the darkness this world provides."

"I'll teach you how to do spells and which ones to stay away from ever trying because they'll bring black magic and terrors to your door." Kelly gave her a crystal tied to a string. "This is for locating spells. And the easiest to learn. You'll be able to find most anything once you learn this locution spell."

Donna handed Mia a black orb. "This is a focusing stone. But it's also a stone for calling one of us if you ever find yourself in trouble and need our help. I'll be teaching you about how to protect yourself against the evil things that'll try and turn you or even hunt you."

Eve moved to get a small box from a desk drawer

and handed it to her daughter. The box contained the necklace of a cat in a regal feline pose. "I get premonitions. I saw your companion would be a feline, so I got you this blessed pendant. It's more than just a trinket though. You'll be able to converse with each other when you're wearing the necklace by just thinking and without vocalizing. It's a conduit for the two of you, but remember, it only works when you're wearing the necklace. This will allow you to talk to him and not look like you're going mental. It will also allow you to converse mentally over a greater distance."

Mia examined all her gifts. She was in awe of everything and thanked each one in turn. After she hugged her mom for her gift, Mia sat back down. "Are my powers available yet? What kind do I have?"

"Tell me, do you ever see or feel anything out of the ordinary? Feel like something happened but you can't prove it wasn't that way to begin with? Has anything unusual specifically happened today?" Donna leaned forward with her sock monkey in hand, waiting.

"Besides a cat talking to me? Not specifically, I don't think. However, I know there are times when I'm feeling anxious or nervous. Like today, I felt something important was about to happen, but I didn't know what.

Do you mean something like that?"

Donna leaned back and smiled. "Exactly like that. Seems you're going to follow your mother in the premonition department. However, this doesn't mean that's the only thing you'll be able to do. Powers take time to develop, but you have one and we can work on building that power while we wait for others to manifest themselves."

"I'll be helping you with premonition, as will your mom. There are also certain tests to see what else you might have. Although with spells and potions you'll be able to do quite a bit. Having powers will just make certain things natural, like breathing. Once, of course, you learn what they are and how to control them." Kelly looked at her watch.

Marion rolled her eyes at Kelly's time keeping. "We'll be going soon enough, Kel. Don't be rushing us." She turned to Mia. "I'm sure this is a lot to grasp all at once. It's already been an emotional day with your dad and all, but please know, we're not asking anything of you right now. We just wanted to welcome you into the coven and prepare you for what you're going to be facing in the days ahead. Everything will happen in its own time."

Chapter Six

"You were rather quiet downstairs," Mia commented as she closed her bedroom door. The night had been busy, full of revelations and surprises.

"I'm rather flabbergasted by the whole enchilada, kitten. And the wine has affected me a bit more than I expected."

"Yeah. It's a lot to take in. This whole day has been. Hearing you talking to me, finding out I'm a witch from a long line of witches, that I'll have powers, plus Dad being taken in for questioning over the deaths of the Hennessys. I know Mom's freaking about that, as well as concerned whether the restaurant can even succeed now. Everything they had was put into the business. After opening night, I thought we were going to be a huge success, but now?" Sitting on the bed, her legs tucked under her, Mia put her head in her hands.

Gumshoe jumped on the bed and rubbed his soft furry body against her arm. *"We'll figure everything out. I can help."*

"How?" Her muffled voice came through her hands and he could tell her word was mixed with tears. What she'd gone through today would be rough on anyone, but she was still young, trying to cope with the unimaginable.

"I don't remember much, but I know I used to be a private investigator. A gumshoe. It's one of the few things I seem to know and how I got my name. In the 1800s, shoes were made of a gum rubber. Later, the term meant to sneak around, at first as a thief, but then as a private detective. I remember being fascinated with the word and decided as a child I'd wanted to be a dick just to have the title of gumshoe."

Pulling her hands from her face, she stared at him. "You were once a child? Once human?"

"Sure thing, baby doll. I remember that much at least."

"What else do you remember?"

Gumshoe thought about it for a couple of minutes. *"Not a whole lot. Honestly, it wasn't until recently I became consciously aware and realized I was even a cat."*

"Really?"

"Yep. I just woke up and I was shorter and furrier with no recollection on what happened or how I got to be this way."

"What's the last thing you remember?"

"Kissing my wife and baby daughter good night and leaving the house."

"You were married? With a family?" Mia was incredulous.

"I was, but it was a long time ago."

"How long?"

"I'm not really sure. I know things are a lot different now, especially the speech, clothes and cars. Everything's different than the few memories I have."

"You just woke up being a Siamese cat?"

"Is that what I am? Siamese?" Gumshoe looked around and saw a mirror on the closet door. Hopping off the bed, he meandered over to look at his reflection. A dark mask around his nose and eyes, as well as dark fur on his paws and tail. The rest of his fur was a tawny color, but what stood out the most were the rich, blue color of his eyes. He twitched his ears, tilted his head and looked down at his tail. *"I wondered what I looked like. A lot different than seeing the man I once was gazing back at me. I wish I could remember more, but even if a man did stare back, I'm not sure I'd recognize him. Everything is just outside my grasp of comprehension in remembering anything significant."*

"I'll help you if I can."

Gumshoe looked up at his new companion. The girl was young, youthfulness displayed on her face. Yet, there was a maturity and determination he was impressed by. She didn't have the beauty of some sexy pin-up girl, but beauty didn't come solely from appearance. To him, it never mattered what color her hair or eyes were, if she was super thin or overweight, if she wore glasses or not. Mia liked to wear thick glasses and baggy clothes, but somehow Gumshoe knew she'd grow out of that when she became more confident in her own appearance. She had a beauty that came from within; her kind heart and caring and compassionate ways made her more beautiful than some of those sexy pin-up broads he used to admire. If the woman was black-hearted with little to no morals, not caring about others less fortunate, it wouldn't matter what her outwardly appearance was. She'd be hideous. *"And I'll help you clear your dad's name. I don't think he purposefully poisoned the Hennessys. Doesn't seem to me he has a reason to. So, either it was a colossal mistake, or someone is shifting the blame on him. And either way, you're not at fault."*

"In the meantime, I'll keep a journal of what you remember. When we get some detail, I'll search the web and we can see what happened to you and your family. If worse comes to worse, we can always go to Plainview and check the county records."

"I'd really appreciate it. Filling in the blanks of my memory would make things better. I hate this not knowing or having these holes in my head of missing time. Besides, working on your case will give me the feeling of being useful again, even if I'm not in human form to do it."

"Then it's a deal." She stood. "I'm going to get ready for bed. Do you want anything while I'm gone?"

"No. I'm peachy."

Mia opened the bedroom door just as the bell rang. She had been expecting her dad to come home, but so far, he hadn't. For a split second she thought maybe it was him and he didn't have his key. She ran down the stairs but stopped short when Eve opened the door to reveal Detective Hardy.

Chapter Seven

Eve was holding Maddie, who was struggling to get down and crying. Bouncing her youngest daughter on her hip, she frowned at Phil, looking behind him for her husband.

"I'm sorry, Eve. I really thought I'd be releasing Adam tonight, but unfortunately, we had to place him under arrest for manslaughter."

"Under arrest? Why?"

"There's been a new development. Katie Arino passed away about two hours ago from mushroom poisoning."

Katie was only nine years old. Her sister, Cathy, was part of Mia's squad. Mia knew Cathy's sister had been one of the people out sick, along with Cathy herself, but she didn't think much more of it until now. After all, Cathy was back in school today and even helped to celebrate her birthday. Cathy and her family must be devastated. Mia felt Gumshoe move beside her, listening in.

"And sadly, it's just not the Arino kid. We have 54 cases of the poisoning. We've had to put a call out to any who ate the soup to go immediately to the hospital."

"What's happening to them?"

"The CDC is taking over their cases until further notice. Seems mushroom poisoning is wicked, making you feel like you have the stomach flu for the first 48 hours. Then you start to feel better, just weak with some of the flu-like symptoms hanging around. What it's doing, though, is working through the system and degrading the organs to the point they fail, causing death. About a dozen folks are having to go through kidney dialysis to flush their bodies of the toxin. Others are also going through a toxin flush, whether having their stomach pumped and hope it hasn't destroyed their organs or having their blood replaced with multiple heavy doses of charcoal to prevent further toxin absorption. A few are on the list for a liver transplant, but there is no antidote, no total cure. Unfortunately, all of them are having to go through treatment of some kind to prevent any further deaths. I had no choice, Eve."

Eve bounced Maddie more, trying to shush her. Mia moved the rest of the way into the foyer with plans to take Maddie from her mother's arms and try to calm her sister down. However, when Mia went to reach for Maddie, Phil stopped her.

"I'd like to ask you some questions, Mia. Mind if I

come in, so we can talk?"

Mia gave her mother a questioning glance, but Eve stepped back. "You two can talk in the living room. I'm going to take Maddie upstairs and get her to bed." Without another word, she headed up the staircase.

Phil rubbed his forehead. "I've a feeling your family won't forgive me easily. I'm just doing my job, Mia. I hope you understand."

"I do, Phil. Come on in." Mia turned and led the way to the living room. She waved at the couch while she occupied the chair opposite. Gumshoe sat at her feet, his tail curled around his paws.

Once they were all settled, Phil took out his notepad to jot down whatever Mia told him. "You were the one who made the soup?"

"Yes. It was my own creative recipe. I saw one for a five-onion soup and altered it slightly for the mushrooms."

"Why not stick with the onions?"

"We already had a French Onion soup on the menu and I thought something different and special would be nice for the opening. Plus, it went better with my whole course. Dad let me plan one full course for the menu."

"What all did that consist of?"

"The five-mushroom soup as my starter. Then I had a pan-seared duck breast served with a blood-orange sauce, citrus-and-bacon-roasted Brussels sprouts, twice-baked sweet potatoes with caramelized pecans, and a chocolate crème Brule."

"I had most of that. I don't care for mushrooms, so opted for the French Onion. The meal was wonderfully delicious. Were you with your father most of the day?"

"I was with him all day."

"Describe the day to me."

Mia thought for a moment before she began. "We got up early and headed to the farmers' market. After getting some fresh donuts for breakfast, we walked through. Dad and I picked the vegetables we wanted for our menu that day and made arrangements to have them delivered about ten, so everyone could start prep. We were at the market until about 8:30 or 9. Then we had a couple more stops to make just outside of town. Mr. Johnson's dairy farm for fresh cream, milk and cheese. Then over to Mr. Hopkins for the delivery of some fresh trout. We were back at the restaurant about 9:45. The deliveries we had scheduled earlier began arriving and everyone started with washing the vegetables and working on general prep. Mom and Dad met with the servers about 2 to go over the menu and by 4 we were officially open."

"Did you meet with Mr. Meyers or someone else for the mushrooms?"

"Mr. Meyers. He's the only local supplier I'm aware of and his product has always been good. He's a mycologist and has been for a long time. I'm sure he didn't sell us a bad product. It doesn't make any sense."

"Mycologist?"

"Expert on mushrooms."

"Ah. Did anyone else have access to the mushrooms after they were delivered to the restaurant?"

"No one other than our staff. Henry washed them for me, but other than that, they were on my station drying, being cut up, or utilized within the soup. By the way, Dad and I both tasted the soup before it went out for service. Neither of us got sick."

"That's because you only tasted it. You didn't actually eat it. Was there any left over?"

"No. It was the first thing we 86ed. It was totally gone within a couple of hours. I couldn't believe how quickly it went."

"Mr. Meyers is missing. Do you have any idea where he might be?"

"I know he does his own hunting for mushrooms, sometimes taking a trip out of town to get them, but I don't know where he goes or how long he goes for. I know he gets some of his mushrooms just outside of town, but as I said, he's an expert on what to harvest, where to find them and what's poisonous. He once took me to pick mushrooms, but I mostly only know him from the farmers' market."

"What about the Hennessys? What do you know of them?"

"They own a cow that's always being tipped over. They live on the edge of town in that little house with the white picket fence and large rose bushes. I know they're in their 70s and they have a couple of kids who don't live 'round here." Mia shrugged her shoulders. "That's about it, I guess."

Phil wrote down everything she said before turning back to her. "Not much of a birthday for you. I'm sorry. Thanks for taking the time to talk to me."

"Will you be able to help Dad? Did anything I tell you help?"

"I'm not sure. It certainly didn't hurt. I know I'm missing something. Someone had access to those mushrooms, either before they were delivered or after.

And I wonder who has it in for your dad and his blossoming business. Do you have any thoughts on who might not want your dad to succeed?" Phil knew that children were often overlooked but would soak up the most minute things. Mia could've seen or overheard something none of the adults noticed.

Racking her brain, she twisted her hands in her lap nervously. "The only one that's possible might be Earl, the owner of the Rocks. He wasn't too thrilled Dad left and took Dominic. He also didn't seem super happy about Jeremy, Dad's old sous chef, becoming the new head chef. However, Earl did stop by before we were open to wish Dad luck on his venture."

"Earl Dapper was in the restaurant during prep?"

"Yeah. He and Dad talked, but they weren't near any of our stations."

"How did he get in? Wasn't the restaurant locked?"

"The front was, but the back was unlocked because we were going in and out with the deliveries and garbage."

"Could he have messed with the food? Could someone else have entered when you weren't looking?"

Mia thought about it. They were all running around so much, somehow it hadn't seemed possible, but the impossible was attempting to make itself plain. "Earl had no chance to mess with the food. He stood in the center of the kitchen almost the entire time. As for someone else entering and us not noticing? Possibly, though I doubt it. We were all running around, focusing on our stations, our work, but I can't believe someone we didn't recognize who wasn't supposed to be there could have entered and left without being observed. You've seen the kitchen. There aren't that many places to hide."

"True. I just thought maybe. Do you think it might be an inside job? How well do you know the other chefs?"

"No. Dad picked them out personally and everyone knew it was a stepping stone to work for him. Have you talked to the other chefs?"

"Yes. You were the last I needed to interview from the kitchen staff." Phil stood. "I'm going to do what I can to get your dad released. I know he's innocent."

"I'll help you in any way I can, Phil. Do anything you need me to do."

"I know you will, but I need you to stay out of trouble and just be the support your folks need right now. I've a feeling it's going to get worse before it gets better." Phil headed towards the foyer and looked up the empty staircase before he turned to Mia. "Tell your mom I said I'm trying my best and to get some rest."

"I will." Mia shut and locked the door behind him, turning out the foyer lights.

Gumshoe walked beside her up the stairs. *"What do you think of that dope?"*

"Phil is not a dope. He's very intelligent and I know he'll work hard to help my dad out. They've been friends since high school." Mia gave him a puzzled look.

"I didn't mean the man. I meant the information the flatfoot just told us."

"Ah. Dope is information and flatfoot, I guess, is cop. For me, dope is good, or with regards to a person, a dummy. However, I think he's right in that it's going to get worse before it gets better. I just wish I knew what to do to help. Plus, I'm shook about Katie. I can't believe she's gone. She's so young. Just doesn't seem possible."

"Indeed. Parents are supposed to kick the bucket before their kids. It's not natural when children die first." Gumshoe thought of his own parents. Suddenly, he remembered his father died during the war. Stress over the concern for his son fighting against a powerful enemy, and an over-indulgence in fatty foods and

cigarettes, caused him to have a heart attack. However, his mom, as much as he could remember, was still alive. Or was when he was still human. So many things were still cloudy, shrouded in the mists of obscurity. *"I remember something. I was in a war and my father kicked when I was overseas fighting."*

"That's great. Every little bit of information helps. I don't mean it's great he died, just that you remembered something. I've never really been exposed to death yet. Other than the old dying of natural causes. Lately though, the news is full of kids my age dying. Some of stupidity, like drugs or drinking and driving. Even if they are sober, they get hit by a drunk driver and pass away." Mia sat on the bed, looking a bit melancholy. "Worse are the recent attacks of guns being brought into schools and the kids being shot, usually at random. Our school is having a protest on Saturday. We're Marching for Our Lives, along with several thousand kids around the country."

"I've not heard anything about this. But then, technically, my cognizant thoughts are only a few days old. You mean to tell me guns are being brought to school? By other kids?"

"Sometimes. Especially if the kids have been

bullied, they think it's a way to protect themselves. And the bullies are there for various reasons: racial, religious, or just because they want to be mean. There're also adults, though, who just burst into schools and shoot them up. Lots of schools around the country have had shootings, bomb threats, and more. Lately, it's been getting worse and the government appears to be more interested in protecting the right to carry arms and the overall gun law instead of protecting those of us in school. But we're also marching for other reforms too. Not just guns, but to get better assistance with mental health. Suicide rate for teens is at an all-time high. I know that this one march isn't going to make much of a difference, but it's a start. It's telling our local and state government we're going to do something to protect our schools. We're there to learn and shouldn't have to be worried about if we're going to live another day."

"I hadn't realized the dangers you've had to face on a daily basis."

"I once thought we were lucky being in a small town. Everyone knows most everyone else, but small towns seem to be where the mass shootings are occurring more than the larger cities. According to something I read before we planned on this project, 63%

of the mass shootings occur in small towns. It's frightening. This march is letting our voices be heard and will hopefully lead to a clear step towards reform. Regardless, being killed by mushrooms is not something that was on my radar. It just seems so impossible. So unreal."

"I'm not sure I can do anything about the mass shootings, or bombs or bullying, but you might when you gain in your powers. However, as for Katie? We can solve that mystery together and hopefully clear your dad as well."

Mia nodded. "Thank you. Any direction is going to help. I'm so lost over this whole thing, I don't know where to begin."

"I don't remember much of my previous life, baby doll, but my job as a private dick. That I think I might've been pretty good at my job."

"Maybe too good, since you can't remember your death either. "

"You may be right. You promised you'd help me discover what happened."

"I know. And I will. As soon as this case is solved, and you remember more solid details to look up."

"Then we better get some rest. We've a lot to

investigate tomorrow."

Mia went into the bathroom and shut the door to prepare for bed. When she returned, she climbed under the covers. "Gumshoe? I'm glad I met you today. You're pretty cool."

"Ain't so bad yourself, kitten. I'm glad too. It's nice to know I have a purpose again instead of just looking for mice." He snorted, then curled up into a small ball of fur at her feet, tucking his tail around his body, his nose under his paws. In moments, he was sound asleep, a soft snore coming from his tiny body. Mia smiled. Just great. Leave it to her to get a snoring, drinking and smoking cat as her companion.

Chapter Eight

"You have a half day today, right?" Eve put a plate of scrambled eggs and toast in front of Mia when she sat down at the kitchen table. It didn't escape her notice how tired her eldest daughter looked and she worried current circumstances affected Mia's sleep.

"Yeah. The squad and I are supposed to work on our posters for the march tomorrow." Although her poster was mostly finished, and she had other things planned for the day, she didn't want her mom to know.

"Can I march too?" Maddie rocked slightly in her booster chair as she ate her cereal.

"That's up to Mom, but it's fine with me. You'll have to make your own poster, though, but I can help you tonight."

"That march affects both of you. We can all be a part of it. Make a stand. I'll help Maddie with her poster, though, Mia. You've got enough to do at the moment."

"Any word about Dad?"

"Where's Daddy? When's he coming home?"

Eve shook her head as she brought a cup of coffee to the table. "No word since last night. I'm sure Phil is doing everything possible to get him out, at least on bail, but it's still a waiting game."

"And the restaurant? What's going to happen with that?"

Gumshoe jumped on the counter and sat, his tail furiously swishing behind him. "Meow!"

"Can Gumshoe have coffee?"

Eve nodded. "I guess. How does he want it?" She stood and got a bowl mug from the cabinet they usually used for soup and poured the feline a quarter cup.

"Mew. Meow, meep, mew mew."

"He says he remembers liking it black, but now a bit of cream would be nice."

Eve got the milk from the fridge and poured some into the bowl with the coffee, putting the whole thing on the floor and out of Maddie's sight.

"As for the restaurant? I don't know. Right now, I guess we're going to stay closed and hope all of this gets resolved quickly, but without your dad to run the kitchen, I don't see any other option."

"I could do it. I can plan the menu and shop. Dad showed me how."

"I'm sure you can, sweetie, but I'm not sure anyone would come to eat there anyways. They are either still recovering or don't trust us."

Mia frowned, picking at her eggs. She knew how much both her parents invested in the business.

Eve didn't want to admit the mushroom affair potentially ruined them. As a parent, she'd protect her children as best as she could. "Did you sleep okay? You look tired."

"Yeah, Mom. I was just..." She threw Maddie a sidelong glance before she continued, "practicing with some of my new birthday gifts from yesterday. I was anxious to try them out and woke up really early." In particular, Mia worked with the locution stone, testing to see if she could figure it out from the extremely brief lesson she'd had when she obtained it.

Breakfast became solemn after Eve's comment. Even Maddie in her Wonder Woman get-up ate quietly and wasn't her usual babbling self. Eve had dark circles under her eyes, indicating she hadn't gotten much sleep. Mia couldn't imagine anyone who had such disregard for her family as to put them out of business and ruin her family's reputation.

This morning, before coming down for breakfast, Gumshoe came up with a plan of what to investigate. He'd go to the Hennessys' while she was at school. Since it was only a half day, he'd meet up with her afterwards and then, together, they'd go see if they couldn't figure out what happened to Mr. Meyers, or at least where he might have gone. From there, they'd see what else they could find, hoping that either or both places would give them some clues on where to continue.

Mia was running everything through her head and was grateful when breakfast was over. Scooping up her book bag, she realized she hadn't opened the gift from Detective Hardy. Tearing the paper, she opened the long thin box to reveal a silver charm bracelet with several kinds of charms relating to her cooking on it. One was a chef's hat, another a rolling pin. There was a butcher's knife, a bowl with a spoon sticking out, and finally a charm that spelled out "#1 Chef." It was beautiful, and she knew the detective was doing the best he could for her family, and especially for his long-time school friend.

"Laters," she called to her mom and headed for the door leading her to the garage where she stored her bike.

"Mia?"

She stopped with her hand on the door knob to face her little sister. "Yeah?"

"You going to Cathy's house after school?"

"Probably not. We're probably just going to work on the posters at the library. Cathy's family is probably not up for company since her little sister is gone."

"What happened to Katie?"

"Why don't you talk to Mom about it?"

"Why?"

"Because I think she can explain better than I can."

"Will you need my lasso, today?"

Mia smiled. Maddie was so into Wonder Woman, she really thought the gold-colored rope she carried on her belt would make anyone entangled within tell the truth. "No, sis."

"Why?"

"You keep it in case you have to protect Mom."

"Why?"

"Because we need to make sure Mom stays safe, so Dad doesn't need to worry about us on top of everything else going on. And please don't ask why again. I'm going to be late for school if I don't go now."

"Okay." Maddie stood with her hands on her hips, her cape over her shoulders. Even Mia had to admit she was cute.

"Meow." {*Time to take a powder.*}

Mia was about to say, "A what?" Then assumed he

was telling her it was time to go and stopped herself from speaking out loud. She knew Maddie was suspicious enough as it was about Gumshoe and his drinking coffee, or being able to understand that he even wanted coffee with cream. She could also tell Maddie was about to ask her about the cat, and those were answers she wasn't quite ready for just yet. Dashing out the door and securing it behind her, Mia took a few moments to find the old bike basket she used to have. Fastening it to the handles, she got on and told Gumshoe to get into the basket so they could take off.

Mia headed towards the school. As they rode along, she pointed down Carnation Boulevard. "The Hennessy house is that way about eight blocks. They're the last house on the street before it turns into a dirt road. It's a small place with a white picket fence. You'll see the barn in the back and their one cow."

"While you're in school, I'll do my best to scope the joint out. See if there's any clues about. It could be the Hennessys were the actual targets and your dad is just the fall guy."

"I know you mentioned that last night, but the Hennessys have been here for a long time. I can't imagine why anyone would want them dead, especially in such a bizarre way. There're a multiple amount of ways that'd be more effective and quicker."

"Maybe your dad is a patsy they wanted as well. Someone they could take down without killing them."

"And that brings us back to why anyone would want to harm my dad and our family."

"Stop this bathtub and I'll go check it out."

Mia pulled over and waited for Gumshoe to hop out of the basket. "Never heard it called a bathtub before."

"That's what we called the bucket alongside a motorcycle in my day. Actually, I think this basket was worse."

"E.T. didn't seem to mind."

"E.T.? Who's that?"

Mia laughed. "Extra-Terrestrial. A movie about an alien who is befriended by a kid and the alien rides around in a bicycle basket. It's an old movie."

"A movie? I've never heard of that movie."

"We can watch it one day, if you want. It's Gucci. I think you'll like it."

"Is Gucci the producer?"

"No. It means it's good."

"I thought good was dope."

"It is. They both are."

Gumshoe put his front paw over his eyes. *"This language thing is going to be interesting."* Putting his paw down, *"I'll get the dope on the Hennessys. See you later, gator."* Turning, his tail in the air, he began walking down Carnation Boulevard.

Mia watched him a moment. "Yep. It's going to be interesting, that's for sure." She continued pedaling towards Midlands High School.

Chapter Nine

For a feline with shorter legs than a human, it took Gumshoe a little longer than he thought it would to get to the end of the paved road and the little white cottage that belonged to the Hennessys. It was a cute place, something his wife would like. Would've liked. He was still getting used to being this way, despite that whatever had happened to him occurred years ago, as well as waking up in this body. He knew cats had nine lives, but he hadn't thought his human existence would be one of them.

The good thing about being a cat was no one really paid attention to him as he skulked around the building. He jumped on a garbage can and climbed up to the window to peer in. Getting inside would be more difficult in this form. As he gazed through the window, he was surprised at how ransacked the place looked.

Before he could give it any more thought, he heard the backdoor slam and running footsteps. Jumping gracefully off the garbage container, Gumshoe ran around to the back just in time to see a thin, hooded figure climb into a sedan and speed off, leaving a cloud of dust from the dirt road in his wake. Although

Gumshoe got a glimpse of him, he didn't recognize him or know who the intruder was.

So, Mia was right. There was something more going on than just a mistake of poisonous mushrooms getting into the restaurant and being served. For a baby doll, she had pretty good instincts.

Although Gumshoe couldn't get the license plate, he did get a decent glimpse of the man. Better yet, he also got the scent of the scoundrel. Nearing the fence, Gumshoe noticed a couple of drops of blood by the gate. Barely noticeable, he knew his feline senses as well as his proximity to the ground accounted for his fortune in finding it.

From the scent, it was different than the one they found at the restaurant behind the dumpster. What was this rat looking for? Did he find it? Who was he? He was sure, in such a small town, he'd see him again, but it'd be nice to know who he was beforehand.

Gumshoe nosed around the building, looking for any way he might be able to squeeze inside. Although, if the man who broke in found what he was looking for, there'd be nothing to find, and if he didn't, then whatever he was searching for most likely wasn't here. At any rate, he was too late to the party for any real clues. Except for the blood. He'll have Mia call the flatfoots to come out and discover it.

Since it was also an official crime scene, Gumshoe felt it prudent not to walk about inside, although that was only what he told himself since he couldn't achieve access to the building. Even paw prints could affect the results. He looked through the window again. Papers were everywhere, drawers tipped over, their items scattered about the rooms. In the corner he spotted a bottle of whiskey and licked his whiskers. He could really use one of those now. Maybe even two or three. And a cigarette. At least he had his morning coffee, which helped to wake him up. Sighing to himself, he turned away and headed towards the restaurant, hoping he'd see the mysterious man along the way. After a short break there, he'd head to the high school to meet Mia. There was a lot of work yet ahead and she should be out of school soon.

Although Gumshoe spent some time walking up and down Main Street, as well as Oak and Sycamore, he didn't see or sense anyone he recognized. When he returned to Main Street to head towards the Midlands High School, he passed by the restaurant, overhearing an argument.

With quickened steps, he headed to the back alley in hopes of discovering what the argument was about and whom it was between. The back door to the restaurant was opened slightly and Gumshoe sprinted inside, tucking himself into a corner so as not to be seen. Eve was there in the center of the room, the other cooks in a circle around her. Dominic was furious, slamming his hand on one of the prep tables.

"This is outrageous! Do you have any idea what I gave up in order to take this job?" Dominic snarled.

"And do you have any idea what we risked to put this restaurant in business? My home as collateral. I gave up my old job and so did Adam. We have no funds coming in. We have a loan we can no longer pay, much less the bills that're going to happen. So don't tell me how awful this is for you. We're about to lose everything." She took a deep breath to calm down and lower her voice to a more reasonable level of discussion. "Look. Detective Hardy is doing his best to clear this up, and as soon as it does, and our name is cleared, we'll reopen. But no one is going to come when they have concerns we're serving food that's killing people. The CDC officially shut us down while they are doing their investigation. Until we're cleared, we aren't open for business. There's nothing I can do. I can only suggest you try and find another job to get money coming in and hope that you'll come back when we're allowed to reopen."

"This is bullshit and you know it!" Dominic slammed his fist against the table again.

The other cooks and servers stood around, mumbling to each other, but no one looked overly surprised the restaurant was closing. Maybe they saw the writing on the wall, or just didn't sympathize with what the Thomas family was going through. Gumshoe hoped it wasn't the latter. He'd gotten the distinct impression Adam chose each and every one of the restaurant crew personally, and to think the crew didn't care one iota whether or not he failed was disheartening.

Chapter Ten

The school bell rang loudly, heard both inside the classrooms and hallways as well as outside on the school lawn. Gumshoe knew he was right on time as the school doors swung open with a loud metal clack and teens poured forth, as if from some volcano spewing its lava along the concrete walkway and over the green grass. Individuals walked hurriedly in one direction or another. Couples and small groups seemed to linger more, talking as they walked away from the impressive red-brick building.

Gumshoe waited a few minutes before he saw Mia and her group of friends head towards the bike rack. Gumshoe sprinted across the lawn to meet up with her. He had a lot to relate, but he knew she needed a few minutes to disentangle herself from the others.

"It almost seems pointless to do this march tomorrow." Shania leaned down to unlock her bicycle from the iron bar.

"I know it may seem that way, but we can't back out. It's happening all across the country and our voices need to be heard." Lynda shifted her backpack to her other arm.

Tiffany shook her head. "Tomorrow the march and then Sunday the wake for Katie. We can still support Cathy and booster the cause."

"I agree with Tiff. My poster is almost done, and I'll finish it up tonight. I thought we might all chip in a little money to donate to a cause of Cathy's choice in honor of her sister. What do y'all think?"

"Mia! That's a fab idea. I'm Hundo P," Karen exclaimed. "I'm going to stop by Cathy's house later. I'll ask her what cause she wants us to donate to."

"Do you want to take care of the funds then too?" Mia turned to Karen. Since she was going to talk to Cathy, it might be easier to have her work on donations as well. "Maybe others in both Cathy's and Katie's classes would like to donate. I'm sure we can talk to Katie's teacher to help us with her classmates."

Karen nodded. "I know Miss Graham. I'll talk to her about Katie's friends. I'm good with being treasurer for this cause."

"Awesome. That's a load off my mind." Mia saw Gumshoe near the rack and finished unlocking her bike. "I gotta go, but I'll see y'all tomorrow. After the march, maybe we can chillax at the ice cream shop?"

"Sounds like a plan. We'll see you later." Tiffany

and the other girls began to walk towards the library to finish the posters for the march.

Mia pulled the bicycle free from the rack and waited for Gumshoe to jump in. Only when they were headed down Main Street did Mia figure she was safe enough to talk to the Siamese sitting primly in the basket, having forgotten to put on the necklace her mother gave her.

"I want to go by the restaurant first, if you don't mind. I'm curious to see what's going on with the kitchen staff. Did you find anything when you went to the Hennessys' place?"

"Actually, yes. I've lots ta jabber about. First, I was over at the restaurant and your mom closed it. Or rather, she told the staff they were temporarily closed. The CDC shut the gin-joint down until they finish their investigation."

"Oh, no! I knew it was bad from this morning, but I hadn't realized how bad."

"Your mom was pretty upset having to tell the staff. There was one man who was particularly upset though. Big dude with an armful of tattoos."

"That sounds like Dominic, the sous chef. He gave up a solid career to follow Dad here, knowing the opportunities he'd have at the Forbidden Fruit."

"Do you think those opportunities included the possibility of taking over the restaurant if something happened to your dad?"

"I hadn't thought of that, but I also don't think so. Dominic knows he's not ready to run a kitchen just yet. It's why he wanted to work for Dad, so he could learn. I know he wants his own place eventually, but not this soon." Yet, Mia had to wonder. "What about everyone else? Did you get any sense from anyone else?" Mia could see the Forbidden Fruit sign up ahead. It sickened her that the restaurant could be shut down forever. No one would trust her father again as a chef if they didn't clear his name.

"I don't know who everyone was, but overall, most were upset at losing a job so quickly. Although there was one who remained rather stoic the entire time. Albeit, he could just have been in shock and absorbing everything. Hard to say."

As they neared the alleyway and the back of the restaurant, Mia stopped her bike short. She could hear someone talking and they were very upset. Normally she would've just continued, but when she heard "kid killed," she felt it prudent to listen in without them knowing she was there. Getting off her bike, she walked to the corner of the building, which had the stoop she'd been sitting on just the day before, and peeked around the corner.

Gumshoe tilted his head, listening, before he slipped around the corner to see who was talking. The privilege of being a cat was people usually didn't pay much attention to them. *That's the one I told you was acting stoic.*

The man had his back to her, but he was wearing one of the restaurant's chef jackets. His words, though, were very distinct. "No. This isn't what I signed up for. I don't care about the old folks, but the kid was only nine. I didn't sign up for that. Bullshit if you think that kid was collateral damage. I won't be held accountable for it."

There was a pause, an obvious indication he was listening as he paced the alley. Mia knew from the voice who it was, and when he turned to head towards her direction, she confirmed it. The prep chef Henry! Mia quickly ducked back out of sight but continued to listen. Pulling her phone out, she pushed the record button and moved back around to catch him on film. This was the evidence she needed to clear her dad. Now if only she knew who Henry was talking to.

"Look, dude. I agreed to switch out the mushrooms for the death caps. I agreed to making sure extra got into the Hennessys' meal, but only enough were supposed to be in the soup to just make everyone ill, not dead. The Hennessys were the only ones who were supposed to die."

Another pause. Mia felt sick to her stomach at what the conversation entailed.

"Fine. Give me my money and I'm out. I'll see you at the rendezvous." Henry tapped the end call button.

Mia pulled back so quickly to shut off the recorder, she hit a can lying by her bent knee, causing it to roll across the alleyway. She held her breath, fear trickling down her veins at being caught by Henry. After all, if Henry could kill an old, harmless couple so callously, killing her wouldn't be hard.

Hearing the metallic clang, Henry headed in Mia's direction. Gumshoe knew Mia could be found out, so he jumped on the dumpster nearby and meowed loudly, then ran past Henry in the opposite direction and away from Mia. "Stupid cat," Henry exclaimed before following the cat to Oak Street where his car was parked.

Minutes later, Gumshoe was beside Mia.

"Thank you. I thought for sure I was a goner when he started walking this way." Mia stood, getting back on her bike. "I need to get this to Phil right away. It'll prove Dad's innocent."

"Not exactly."

"What do you mean?"

"We can't prove who Henry was gum-flapping to. A one-ended conversation is not enough proof, and we should wait until we know more before we go to the black and whites. It won't hurt to investigate a little more first. Let's get some solid proof and not just what's been recorded by your little gadget. In the meantime, I didn't get a chance to tell you about the Hennessy place. Let's head out that way and I'll bring you up to date."

Mia waited for Gumshoe to get into the basket and get somewhat comfortable before heading back on Main Street towards the school and Carnation Blvd. Turning left, she waited for Gumshoe to talk, but when he didn't say anything, she prodded him. "Well? What'd'ya find out?"

"Sorry. I was looking for the vehicle I saw at the house earlier. Their home had been ransacked. I couldn't get inside, but when I got there, the perp was hightailing it to his vehicle and sped away, leaving a

cloud of dust, so I couldn't get a better look. Thing is, I think he cut himself. There were a couple blood drops by the fence line. Barely visible, so you might have to point them out to the flatfoots."

"Ransacked? What do you think they were looking for? Do you think they found whatever it was?"

"That's uncertain. If they found it, we'll never know what it was. If they didn't, probably means it's not there. Either way, doesn't help us. Do you have any idea what the Hennessys would've had worth killing for?"

Mia shook her head. "I really didn't know them that well. They were just the nice old couple at the edge of town we'd pass on our way to a couple of the farms we'd stop by for dairy, eggs or trout. Occasionally Dad would stop if we saw them in the yard working on their rose bushes, but other than that, I really didn't know them."

"You said last night people would tip their cow?"

"Some of the kids would. They thought it was on fleek to play the prank, but the cow was getting old and I thought it was an awful thing to do to such a gentle creature. As far as I know, though, no one lately has bothered the cow or them."

"Fleek? That's a good thing?"

"Really, Gumshoe. You're behind the times not knowing this stuff. Fleek is great."

"Stop!"

Mia was so startled by the command she braked hard, putting her feet down to steady the bicycle. Looking around to see what caused his sudden demand, she realized there was a car parked just beyond the house.

"Is that the car you saw earlier?" Keeping her voice low, she moved so as not to be seen by anyone in the car.

"No. The style is wrong. I saw a car not a truck, but the fact someone else is at the house is disconcerting. And isn't that Henry's truck? This could be the rendezvous he was discussing on the phone. Which means, someone else could be there and be dangerous."

Mia craned her neck to see. "A beige truck? Yes. Henry drives a beige pick-up. Maybe you're right and this is his meeting spot. Maybe we can see who was on the other end of the conversation that hired him?"

"Let's just stay low until we know for sure." Gumshoe hopped out of the basket and sprinted across the road for a better look.

Mia stashed the bike by some bushes before she

crept low to get across the road. If anyone was watching her, they'd think she'd lost her mind or was up to no good. She didn't care, though. Her father's reputation and her family's source of living were all on the line, and she was bound and determined to do whatever it took to get to the bottom of it all. Together, the two of them crept up to the house, hiding by the garbage cans. The truck was there. "That's Henry's all right," she whispered to Gumshoe. "But I don't see him or anyone he might be meeting."

In the meantime, Gumshoe was looking through the window once again. At first, nothing had changed much since he was there a few hours ago. The place had papers strewn all over, drawers pulled out and dumped, then left upside down. He shifted slightly before he backed up and blocked Mia's view just as she was about to peer in the windows. *"Don't look. Call your friend, the flatfoot, and get him out here. Tell him to bring a meat wagon. You don't need to see what's inside."*

Asking for a meat wagon already told her enough. Someone inside was dead, and since Henry's truck was here, she could only assume it was him. She'd get a look later, but for now, she followed his instructions and pulled out her phone to call Phil.

It took several rings before the detective answered. "Detective Hardy."

"Phil? This is Mia." For some strange reason she was almost shaking with her nervousness.

The tone of her voice must've told him something was wrong. "Mia? Everything okay?"

"No. You need to come to the Hennessy place and bring the coroner. I think Henry's dead."

Although Phil wanted to know why she was there, or Henry for that matter, he didn't ask. "Don't touch anything. I'll be right there."

She snorted. Why in the world would he think she'd touch anything? She wasn't a noob and she watched enough cop shows to know better. Instead, she had Gumshoe show her the place where he saw the drops of blood earlier. She was grateful it hadn't rained and washed the evidence away, but even still, she hoped there was enough there to give them some idea who left the trace evidence behind.

Before she could give it any more thought, she saw the lights of Phil's car approach. It was only moments later the ambulance pulled up behind him.

Phil headed straight for Mia, his eyes full of worry. He'd been a part of the family her whole life and she considered him a beloved uncle. "What are you doing here? Are you okay?"

She nodded. Gumshoe gave her some suggestions on what to say without lying, but also without seeming to interfere with his case.

Phil held her with his arms out, looking her up and down before he released her. "What are you doing here, again?"

With Gumshoe at her feet, she told the story they had worked on. Mostly the truth, she did omit a couple of key points. "I was going to stop by the restaurant on my way home from school. Half day, you know. When I got close, I overheard Henry arguing with someone on the phone and his words caught my attention. I even recorded a bit of it, so you can hear for yourself. He then got into his truck and I decided I would try and follow him, because maybe he'd lead me to the person he was talking to."

"Why did you think that?" Phil was intrigued with the story, but just then, the EMTs called to him from inside the house. "Stay here. We'll finish this up as soon as I take care of what's inside."

Without waiting for confirmation, he headed up the couple of stairs into the back door of the house. She was going to wait, had every intention of doing so, but her curiosity was too strong and she moved to the back door enough that she could see and hear what was going on.

Henry was lying on the kitchen floor with a carving knife embedded in his chest. On top was a piece of paper that she overheard the men say was a suicide note. Like, why would someone commit suicide in a deceased couple's house? Or by plunging a knife in the middle of their chest when there were far easier ways to do the deadly deed? Did the murderer really think they were stupid? Besides, she had the recording of Henry talking to someone about meeting them to get paid. She could only assume this was the rendezvous point they'd discussed on the phone. Of course, the murderer wouldn't know she overheard them. She knew it was important for the killer not to find out, in case they decided she was also a loose end that needed to be dealt with.

It was over an hour before Phil returned outside to talk to Mia. "You said you had video of an argument involving Henry?"

Mia rapidly nodded, cueing up the recording to play for him. As Phil watched and listened, he frowned. He pulled out his notepad and checked it before calling

Officer Easton over.

"Yes, sir?"

"Did we find any cell phones on or around Henry?"

"No, sir. The Hennessys had a landline, though."

"No. Has to be a cell. Have them look around once more and also check his truck."

Mia moved up to Phil. "No cell phone?"

"No. And he obviously had one."

"It's not a suicide, Phil. He was killed, and I'll bet the killer took the phone so we couldn't trace who he'd been talking to."

"Had I not seen your video, I wouldn't have believed it myself. However, that being said, you might be correct in thinking the phone was removed by the killer. I'll pull the phone records and see who he might've called. I'm afraid I'm going to have to keep your phone for a bit. Evidence. I'll get it back to you as soon as possible. You should get home before you make your mom worry." Phil tucked the phone into his pocket, to Mia's dismay.

"What if I need my phone?"

"When I was a kid, we didn't have them, and we managed to live past the stone age. You will too."

"Difference is, in the stone age you didn't have

someone killing people and might come after you."

Phil rubbed his chin as he thought about it. "You've got a point. Is there a way you can copy and send me the file?"

She nodded. "Yep. That I can do."

Phil handed her phone back and she copied the link and sent it to him. Moments later, he confirmed he received it. "This is good evidence proving your father most likely isn't involved. It'll help in getting him released."

She almost tackled him with a hug. "Thank you."

Chapter Eleven

When the questioning was completed and Henry was removed to the medical examiner to be given an autopsy, Mia and Gumshoe headed away from the Hennessy house.

"Where to now?" Gumshoe jumped into the basket on her bike.

"I was thinking maybe we should see if we can find Mr. Meyers. Phil said he hadn't shown up at his house, but I don't see why we couldn't check out a few places on our own. Maybe even find a clue if he was really the one who gave Henry the death caps. If not, maybe he'll have an idea who might've done it. Regardless, I'd like to try finding him and asking him these questions."

"Do you know where he lives? Or where to look for him?"

"Kind of. I'm going to try the location spell using the charm Ms. Lucas gave me on my birthday."

Gumshoe rolled his eyes. Not easy for a feline to accomplish.

"What? I know I had trouble when I first got it, but with the practice, I'm hoping for success." She pulled out a map and the stone charm. She could understand

Gumshoe's hesitation, considering she'd tried to locate her dad the morning after she received it, but she'd only succeeded in having it indicate her home. It took her over an hour of practice before the charm finally indicated the police station. She hoped she'd be more successful this time searching for Mr. Meyers. She also pulled out her notebook for the words she needed to recite, holding the stone above the area map. "Locution, work your charm. Guide me to the one I seek. Keep him from harm until I find him from behind the veil I wish to peek."

The stone started moving, swinging in circles, then dropped on an open area by Highway 31.

"Did it work?" Gumshoe sat up, trying to see where it landed.

"I think so. I have an idea this is where he sometimes likes to hunt for mushrooms. It's not too far out of town. He took me hunting for them once, but I don't remember where the place was exactly. He told me it was a good place to go and why. He actually showed me what to look for in finding the edible mushrooms. That's why I can't imagine he'd be the one to switch them out for poisonous ones. It'd ruin his reputation as much as ours. Let's go see if the spell worked." She pedaled along Carnation Blvd. until she got to Oak. Then, she turned north out of town towards Plainview.

In minutes, the two of them entered a wooded area, indicating they were leaving the limits of Midlands behind. Between Midlands and Plainview was open farmland and wooded areas. Highway 31 connected the two populated areas.

"Have you remembered anything else about your past? Maybe even what war you were involved in?"

Gumshoe shook his head. *"Not really. I remember a lot of explosions going on around me and seeing the bodies of fallen comrades nearby. I can't even tell you who we were fighting, or what their uniforms looked like. Every time I try to remember something, it gives me a headache and I don't succeed in anything but that."*

Gumshoe was just trying to ride out all the bumps in the basket. It sucked not having any thumbs to hold on with and being bounced around. He felt like his teeth should be chattering, even though he was sure cats didn't do that. However, he wasn't going to complain about the transportation. He still appreciated he found someone he could talk to and who was willing to help him as much as she could. It was well worth the discomfort of being tossed about in a basket.

Mia seemed to sense his being uncomfortable in the basket. Tomorrow she'd put a blanket on the bottom for him as a cushion, hopefully making the ride more tolerable. As a feline, he was lean and muscular, so she was sure he was feeling every jolt made by the bicycle. "We're almost there." She pointed to a small, almost hidden trail between the trees up ahead. "For some reason, this part of the woods seems to stay moist and is a good breeding ground for mushrooms. Mr. Meyers comes out here often to collect them. If he can't get them here, he told me he has a couple of other sites he checks out. He'll sometimes stay for a couple of days to hunt them all. He likes to camp, so if he's here, we should see his blue tent nearby. I don't know where his other sights are, so I'm hoping he's here and just isn't aware of what's going on or that the cops are looking for him."

"Or maybe he does, and he's hiding out. We need to be careful."

Once they arrived at the small trail, Mia got off the bike and waited for Gumshoe to jump out. She put the bike behind the bushes, unsure of why she felt the need to hide it. It was that sense she'd been gifted that told her to be more cautious than she normally would. Mrs. Antonio and the others assumed she'll get a couple more powers, but they needed time to develop. She secretly hoped invisibility would be one of them. The idea of walking around her peers in a way they didn't know she was around seemed the coolest ability to obtain.

Gumshoe took the lead down the small trail and she silently followed. She wished she remembered the enchanted necklace her mother had given her so she could talk to Gumshoe without actually vocalizing it. It was going to be the first thing she did when she got home, and she'd never take it off.

"Do you sense anything?" she whispered to him as she continued to look around for any sign that Mr. Meyers was around.

"Someone has been through here recently."

No sooner did Gumshoe respond that Mia noticed the top dome of blue and grey fabric. She pointed. "That's Mr. Meyers' tent." Taking a deep breath, she headed right for it, calling his name.

"Mr. Meyers? It's Mia. Are you in there?" She approached his campsite cautiously, listening for any response. What she got was a bit of gurgling from inside the tent. It didn't sound natural and she suddenly forgot her fear as concern took over. "Mr. Meyers? Are you okay?"

She unzipped the tent, hoping she wouldn't find him in a compromising condition as she peered inside. "OMG! Mr. Meyers?" She ducked inside and knelt alongside the man.

His skin tone was a jaundice yellow, his lips were beginning to turn blue. His breathing was shallow, and she knew he needed medical attention immediately. "I'm going to get help. Just hold on a little longer."

She slipped out of the tent and pulled out her cell phone. It showed only one bar, but she hoped it'd be enough to get help out here. She had so many questions she wanted to ask, but if he died, he might take all the answers with him. She punched in 911 and was glad to hear it answered almost immediately. She gave the best instructions she could, then headed back to the main road to wait for the ambulance crew to arrive so she could show them the rest of the way.

Pacing, she realized Gumshoe didn't come with her. He must still be looking around for any clues as to what might've happened. Something she greatly wondered about as well. Ten minutes later, she saw the ambulance down the road and waved to make sure she got their attention.

The red-and-white vehicle pulled up to her and she

told them Mr. Meyers was down the path. Running ahead of them slightly, the ambulance slowly followed her until they could progress no farther due to the brush. Getting the gurney out, they followed her further into the wooded area where the tent was located. "Wait out here," The EMT ordered, and two of them went inside.

Pacing slightly, she kept trying to peek into what was going on inside the tent. "Is he going to be okay?" she queried as they emerged with the mycologist.

"Unknown at this time. How are you related?" Although he didn't stop, he knew she'd follow him.

"He's a friend. I hadn't seen or heard from him in a few days and thought I'd check up on him."

"Good thing you did. You might've just saved his life."

"Where are you taking him?"

"Midlands General."

Mia held back as Gumshoe joined her. As they watched the men put Mr. Meyers in the back and leave, she could feel a change in the feline. "What's up?"

"I remember. I remember my human name is Alexander."

"Like the ambulance." The sign on the side read Alexander Ambulance Services.

"Yeah. I can hear that name being called. Seeing it must've triggered a memory. My name is Alexander."

"Is that a first name or last?"

Gumshoe paused. *"Not sure."*

"Well, it's a start." She smiled down at him.

"I want to show you something I found before we head to the hospital." Without waiting, Gumshoe returned down the narrow path, only instead of heading towards the makeshift camp he went in the opposite direction. After a decent hike, Gumshoe stopped at an area where there'd been some recent digging.

She wasn't sure what might have been there or what was hidden. Gumshoe started digging in a way that reminded her of a cat in a litter box. In minutes, he uncovered a small black orb and she gasped. Pulling it from the base of the tree, she sniffed it.

"What is it?"

"If I'm right, and I'm not saying I am, this looks like a truffle. Understand, I've only seen pictures of them, so it could just be a lump of fragrant dirt." She brushed it off as best as she could before she stuck it in her pocket. She'd have to use the web to see if she was correct.

"Come on. I want to get to the hospital, and along

the way I want to call Detective Hardy to meet us there. Mr. Meyers needs to be questioned as soon as possible, just in case he doesn't make it."

Chapter Twelve

Unfortunately, felines weren't allowed in a hospital. Gumshoe found a cozy spot where he could keep an eye on her bike and the door for her to come out. Curling up into a small ball, he thought maybe a cat nap might be just the thing he needed to get his insides back in line from being jostled all about in the basket. He'd sense when Mia would come out, and if he fell asleep he knew she'd call for him and that would wake him up.

Mia sat in the waiting room, flipping through Facebook on her phone. All her friends were discussing the march tomorrow. It was important for her to add her voice to such a notable cause, but she worried her attention would be more on this case than on the good of trying to get changes made to protect students going to school.

Phil walked in with Officer Easton and headed right for the nurses' station where the doctor was looking over some medical charts. She knew they'd tell him what was going on, so moved closer to hear.

"He's still unconscious. We had to pump his stomach, but the damage to his liver and kidneys may be irreparable. The poison has also affected his heart. He's on the wait list for a heart transplant just in case the charcoal treatment fails. Even if we find a donor, it might not be worth it with all the other damage his body sustained."

"Any idea how he got the poison into his system? Did he ingest it like the others?"

"No. We thought so at first, but the effects are moving way too rapidly. After we pumped his stomach, we realized the absorption occurred in an alternative way."

"How?" Phil jotted down notes furiously into his pad.

"Unknown at this time. However, I suspect it might've been added directly to his bloodstream, which would account for most of our attempts to cure him failing." The doctor became more stoic than before, a sign for those who knew him to realize he hated admitting he didn't know something.

"Can I speak to him?"

"He's been mostly unconscious with only brief periods of lucidity. You can try, but I wouldn't expect much."

"Thank you, doctor." Phil turned to Easton. "I want a 24-hour watch on him." It was then he noticed Mia standing nearby. "I'm told you found him?" He moved over to the young woman.

"Yes. I got to thinking maybe he was out hunting mushrooms and didn't realize what was going on."

"How did you know where to look?"

"He took me there once a long time ago. I wasn't sure he'd even be there or that I'd remember the spot. In truth, I found it sooner than I thought I would. I remember walking farther into the woods than I did this time, but I was younger then, so who knows? Could be that's where this year's crops were located. Is he going to be okay?"

Phil frowned. "Unsure at this time, but it's not looking too good. I'm hoping to catch him alert enough to answer a couple of questions."

"Can I go in with you?"

The detective was going to say no but decided against it. After all, his best clues came from her and she did find Samuel Meyers. In an uncle fashion, he put his arm around her shoulders. "Just stay quiet and whatever you hear or see in there, don't repeat to anyone else. Not even your mom. Hell, Eve will kill me if she knew how much you're involved in this investigation."

"I won't tell Mom or any of my friends. I won't say

anything. Thank you." She walked beside him down the hall to Sam's private room. The man lying on the bed still looked weak and pale, but the blue color of his lips had dissipated and the jaundice complexion wasn't quite as pronounced. He was hooked up to three IVs and several monitors.

The room was relatively small, mostly taken up by the bed and machines. There was one chair along the wall and a small set of windows on the opposite side. A door led to a bathroom and a small closet held the few personal items he was brought in with. Mostly, his clothing.

Mia moved to the chair to stay out of the way as promised. She'd never seen Mr. Meyers as anything but a robust man who enjoyed the outdoors, until now. It amazed her how frail and weak he appeared lying in the sterile environment.

Phil looked at the monitors for a moment, then slightly leaned over the bed to peer closely at him. "Sam? Are you awake? It's Phil Hardy. Detective Hardy. Can you answer a couple of questions?"

Sam blinked, but one could tell he was having trouble keeping his eyes open. His words were soft and slightly mumbled, mixed with a heavy dose of sleepiness. Mia assumed it was the drugs they gave him to help him recover, or at least feel better.

"I'll try."

"Good. That's good, Sam. Can you tell me what happened to you in the woods?"

"Getting more stock for the market."

"How long have you been out there?"

"Don't know."

"Do you know how you got so sick?"

Sam didn't answer immediately. Mia wondered if he might've gone back to sleep, but then he answered the question, and when he did, she knew it wasn't the truth. He was hiding something, or someone. "Not sure."

Mia wanted to say something, tell Phil he wasn't being honest, but she also promised to remain quiet while in the room. She'd tell him afterwards. He was a good detective, though, and probably already knew Sam wasn't being completely honest.

"Alright, Sam. How about you tell me about the poison mushrooms you picked for the opening night of Adam's restaurant and how you slipped them among the ones you originally sold him?"

"Don't know what you're talkin' 'bout."

"Sure you do, Sam. You're the expert of

mushrooms, and Adam didn't get them from anyone else but you. Strange how someone who loves mushrooms had everything but the mushroom soup at opening night."

Mia blinked. That was news she hadn't been aware of. Did he come in after the soup had already been 86ed? Phil's next statement indicated no.

"You were one of the first people at the restaurant that night, yet you avoided anything that had mushrooms in it. Why? Did you already know they were bad?"

"No." Sam sighed. "Tired."

A nurse came in just as Sam said the last word. "I think that's enough for now, detective. He needs his rest. You can ask him more later."

Phil nodded and looked at Mia before he headed out of the room. She felt it was his way of telling her she could stay and try to get more info out of him if she could. The nurse quickly checked the monitors and drips, then followed Phil out of the room. She sat there quietly, watching the blinking lights of the heart monitor, listening to the beeps of the machines. After several minutes, she moved closer to the bed.

"Mr. Meyers? It's Mia Thomas. I'm the one who found you in the woods. I hope you're going to be okay."

Sam opened his eyes to peer at the young woman. "Thank you."

"I wish I found you sooner. Do you know what's been happening? The restaurant is closed because of mushroom poisoning. We're going to lose everything." She wailed softly.

"I know. I'm sorry. It wasn't meant to be this way."

"What wasn't?"

"Your family suffering as a result..." He stopped midsentence and she knew he wanted to say more.

Take it slow. Don't push him and maybe he will let more of the story slip, Mia thought, her late-night watching of crime shows on Netflix spurring her course of action. She wasn't a professional in interrogation, but she hoped he'd be influenced a bit more easily because he had known her since she was five. "Did you sell us bad mushrooms?"

"No. I sold your father only the best of my stock."

"Then how did we get the bad ones?"

Sam didn't answer, so Mia prompted him further. "Did you give them to Henry?"

Sam looked away, refusing to respond.

"Did you know Henry is dead?"

"Henry's dead?" Sam gasped in disbelief, his eyes flew open as he turned his head back to Mia.

"Yeah. I found him earlier today too. I know he was involved in planting the mushrooms in my soup. I heard him talking to someone about being paid to do so. Was he talking to you?"

Mia didn't think it possible, but she'd swear Sam paled even more.

"No, he wasn't talking to me."

"But you know who he was talking to, right?"

"I've got a good idea."

"Who is it? Is it the same person who did this to you? Are they trying to kill you too, so as to leave no witnesses?"

"Maybe, but I'm not going to tell you and put you in danger too. Forget all this. It's not worth it. Nothing is worth your life."

"I can't, Mr. Meyers. It's my dad's livelihood and the start of mine. I made the soup. Without the restaurant, my family loses everything. How can I forget this?"

"I'm sorry, Mia. I never wanted any of this to happen, especially to you or your family. There's just nothing I can do now, other than to stay quiet and hope no one else gets hurt as a result."

Mia frowned. Remembering the ball of dirt Gumshoe found, she pulled it out of her pocket. "What's this?" She was hoping he'd confirm her suspicions.

"Where'd you get that?" Weak though his voice was, it still radiated with a mixture of anger and concern.

"I found it nearby your camp." She wasn't about to go into details of how it was found, or the fact it was farther from the camp than she'd make him believe.

Sam worked his jaw, an indication of the internal struggle he was having with himself to tell her. Decision made, he answered. "It's a tuber melanosporum."

"What's that?"

Sam sighed. In for a penny, in for a pound. "A black Périgord truffle."

Now she paled. A black Périgord truffle, also known as a black diamond truffle, was worth a ton of money. If Mr. Meyers found a bunch of these, the land that grew them was worth thousands, no, millions of dollars. "This is what you all are after?"

Sam gave a quick nod, then shut his eyes. He was physically and emotionally exhausted.

Mia knew not to push him further. She knew where to look next. County records to see who owned the land the truffles were on. For some odd reason, she had a suspicion of who it might be. "Get some rest, Mr. Meyers. I hope you get well soon. I'll stop by in a day or so and check on you. Would you like me to bring you anything when I do?"

"No thank you, Mia. Very kind of you. But promise me, don't let anyone else know you found that truffle. I don't want you risking your life for something as trivial as money and greed."

"I'll stay safe." Mia looked at the monitors once more before giving him a wisp of a smile, patting his free arm lightly. Heading out of the room, she noticed Officer Easton standing in the hall. "There is a chair inside if you want to get it and sit."

"Thank you. I think I will." He moved inside and moments later came back with the chair to sit in the hallway as guard for the room. With the possible murder attempt on Sam's life, Phil had made sure there was security to keep Sam protected.

Leaving the hospital, she thought she recognized someone approaching Sam's room, but when she looked again to confirm what she saw, he was gone. *Odd,* she thought. Once outside, she called to Gumshoe.

Chapter Thirteen

"Why aren't we telling this to that flatfoot friend of yours?" Gumshoe sat next to her, staring at the computer screen as she typed in a search for county records.

"Because I don't want to go with just a hunch. I want to see if I'm right. I think I have a clue as to some of what's been going on, but I need to make sure before I bring him in on my ideas."

"Seems he could do the work much faster and without issue."

"Yeah, he probably could, but you put me into the investigative mood and I kind of want to finish it." She pulled up property records as well as a map of the area between Midlands and Plainview. It took several minutes to narrow down where the camp was located, and then guesstimated where they found the truffle. She'd done some research and learned black diamonds were found in Hazelnut and Oak Tree groves, both of which were prevalent along that stretch of area between the two towns. It took her several more minutes to pull up the ownership records, and when the result came in, she sat back. "I was right." She pointed to the screen.

"The Hennessys owned the land. They probably didn't know about the truffles there, and someone is after the land to have access to the truffles."

"That's really good gumshoe work, baby doll." He peered closer to look at the actual deed of property.

"Do you understand what you're reading?"

"Most of it. For some reason, natural things, like reading, speaking, knowing how to do things, are easy and in my wheelhouse. It's the personal stuff, like my name and my background, that I'm having trouble with."

"We'll figure it out. I promise." She reached over and rubbed just behind his ears, enjoying the sound of his purring. "So, what do we do now?"

"Now, we get some rest. You've got your march tomorrow. Afterwards, we can talk to the flatfoot and give him everything we know. He can follow up. Let him do his job."

"I'd still like to know who is behind all of this, though. Who else knew about the truffles? Who killed Henry and the Hennessys? Who tried to kill Mr. Meyers?"

"Most likely it's one person behind everything, but what the connection is, is still a mystery."

"Just before I came out of the hospital, I thought I saw someone, but I'm not sure. It was just a brief glimpse. Did you happen to notice anyone unusual about that time?"

"I thought I smelled the person who left the blood behind at the Hennessys' house, but when I looked up, he was gone."

"Then maybe I was right in sensing him in the hospital. He might have gone to finish the job he started with Mr. Meyers. I'm glad Phil left Officer Easton there to guard him."

"Smart move on the flatfoot's part. Might just have saved Meyers' life. Again."

"I sure hope he's going to be okay. He's really a nice man."

"Minus the fact he was in on murdering an old couple, I'm sure he's just the cat's meow."

She puckered her face at him as she pulled her hand back. "Well, I still hope he's going to be okay." Although, Mia had an idea to help Mr. Meyers, and once she returned home, she wanted to speak to her mom. Finding her mother in the kitchen and realizing Maddie was in the back yard playing, Mia sat at the counter and watched her mom prepare dinner.

"Need any help?"

Eve gave Mia a smile, but shook her head. "No. I got this. Have you finished your homework?"

"I did most of it in school. My poster's ready for the march tomorrow. Can I ask you a question?"

Eve wiped her hands and moved to stand across from her daughter. "Anytime."

"Why can't we make a potion or create a spell to cure everyone that has become ill from the mushrooms? Especially Mr. Meyers. The hospital staff don't think he's going to survive. Isn't there anything we could do?"

Eve shook her head. "We told you before, curing something like the poisoning would cause too much alarm from those who were miraculously healed. Plus, it'd throw off the balance of nature. As much as I hate to say it, preventing Katie's death, the Hennessys', or even healing Mr. Meyers would disrupt the natural order of things. Even when that natural order comes from man's greed. You think I don't want to cast some spell so your father would be released and back home with us? To help our business succeed? Doing so is not worth the price that'd have to be paid in the long run." She reached across the counter for her daughter's hand. "I understand how much you want to help. To fix things. It just can't be done in certain situations and this is one of them. If Mr. Meyers suddenly became well again, it'd raise a lot of questions no one would be able to answer, and that'd make it dangerous for us."

"I guess I understand. It's just a shame that we can't do more. He's a nice man. None of them should have died. Especially Katie."

"I agree. There're enough bad things in this world without adding to them." Eve pulled her hand back. "Go get Maddie and both of you get cleaned up. Dinner is almost ready."

GUMSHOE AND THE MYSTERIOUS MUSHROOM

Chapter Fourteen

The morning was bright and sunny, and for just a few minutes Mia wasn't going to think about her dad still being held in custody, or the deaths and illnesses of so many. Today was about another issue entirely. One that personally affected her, her sister and her friends. So far they'd been lucky. Only one bomb threat about two years ago that proved, thankfully, to be false, and no snipers or classmates or any other kind of gunmen to go into the classrooms. That didn't mean the threat wasn't real, for something could happen, and did, in other parts of the country. She hated feeling nervous about going to school every day, wondering if she and her squad would be safe. If at the end of the day they'd have nothing but quizzes, tests, papers and homework to deal with. Her age group shouldn't even be thinking about death daily, when getting an education should be utmost in their minds. Something had to be done and that's what the march was about. A chance for people in school to make a stand to the community and the politicians that something needed to be done to protect them better. Stronger gun laws, stronger investments in their futures.

Grabbing a Pop-Tart and her sign, Mia headed out

the door only to have her mom stop her.

"I'm going to take Maddie. I'll walk with her. You be careful as well. Are you coming home after the march?"

"No. The squad and I are going to the ice cream shop afterwards, and then I need to talk to Detective Hardy about a couple of things. Have you heard from him? Any news about Dad coming home?"

"Not yet. Although he did say he was getting evidence to prove your father had nothing to do with the poisoning, there are still some unanswered questions, and it's because of this they are still holding him. What did you need to tell Phil?"

"I might have some information proving Dad isn't involved, but I need to talk to him about it before I say anything to anyone else."

Eve looked at her eldest, physically biting her lip. "Alright. Just don't get into trouble. I couldn't handle that on top of your father."

"I won't, Mom. I promise. See ya later, Maddie." Without further ado, she dashed out the door, Gumshoe on her heels. This time she had a small blanket and stuffed the basket with it in order to give him a bit more cushioning while he rode.

She was meeting her friends at the school so headed that way, taking Rose Street to Main to the school grounds.

"Thanks for the blanket. It makes riding this bathtub not as bumpy as before."

"I'm sorry I didn't remember to do something yesterday."

"You've got a lot going on, so it's understandable. I'd never ridden in a bucket before, so I didn't know how it'd be."

"Are you going to walk with us in the march?"

"I thought I would, if that's okay. Maybe I can pick up the scent of the unknown behind everything. Or maybe even see the vehicle from the Hennessys' yesterday."

"I can't believe how much has happened in just a day's time. First the Hennessys' place trashed. Oh, I'll bet they were looking for the deed to that grove where the truffles are!"

"That'd make sense. When we talk to the flatfoot, we can make sure he's on the lookout for a transfer of title. Whoever has the land deed would be the one who's behind all of this. And they can convict him with that DNA sample they got yesterday at the fence."

"How do you know about DNA?"

"Heard the flatfoots talking about it. Figured it out."

"Anyways, after the Hennessys, the convo with Henry on the phone and then finding him dead, then finding Mr. Meyers and the truffles, I feel like I lived a week just in that one day."

"How do you think I feel? I've only been conscious of being a human for this past week. It's a lot to take in."

"I see everyone up ahead." She waved at her friends, who had been watching for her arrival. She stopped near them and they gathered around.

"That cat seems to really like you. You taking him everywhere with you now?" Lynda wiped her mouth of the banana she was eating with the back of her hand.

"Yes. He's my new companion and likes to be where I am. His name's Gumshoe."

"Funny name," Cathy commented.

Mia put the kickstand on, then hugged Cathy. "I'm so very sorry to hear about Katie."

Cathy hugged her then pulled back. "Thanks."

Mia was grateful Cathy didn't appear to hold any ill-will towards her, since it was the mushrooms that made both sisters ill and eventually took Katie's life. "You know, we're learning more about what happened and who's really behind it. They're going to catch everyone involved and it'll prove me and my dad had no knowledge of it."

"Your dad's the head of the kitchen. Shouldn't he and you know what ingredients you use? Shouldn't you have noticed something was wrong?" Okay, so maybe Cathy wasn't as forgiving and understanding as originally thought.

Mia nodded. "In reality, yes. And we purchased all the right ingredients that morning from the farmers' market. However, yesterday we learned Henry, one of the line cooks, snuck the poison into my broth without any of us knowing."

"Why would he do that?" Shania twirled a bottle of water as she listened, her sign leaning against her thigh.

"Seems someone paid him to do it. I overheard him talking to someone that he wasn't up for being involved in Katie's death or the sickness of so many people. He argued with them on the phone and then demanded he be paid. I tried to follow him, but by the time I caught up, he was dead."

"Dead?" Karen gasped.

"Yeah. Stabbed in the chest. See, Cathy. My dad and me aren't responsible. We couldn't predict Henry being bought off to poison people, nor could we know that doing so would take innocent lives. You've got to know we'd never do anything like that."

"Yeah. Deep down I knew, I'm just upset." Cathy's eyes welled up with unshed tears.

Mia moved over to her again. "I know you are. I am too. Katie was a sweet kid and taken from us far too soon."

"Which is one of the reasons we're doing this march. Not for poison mushrooms, but for the safety and security of all of us teens and kids. We're lining up," Karen pointed out.

"I'm going to lock up my bike and I'll join you all in a minute." Mia pushed back the kickstand and walked the bike over to the rack. She noticed Gumshoe stayed where the others were, but she'd rejoin all of them in a couple of minutes. She locked up her bicycle, grabbed her sign, and started to walk around the corner to where she left her companions.

Mia didn't pay attention to the car that pulled up behind her, nor the person getting out. She was too focused on catching up to her squad for the walk and many parents were dropping their kids off to join in. However, when she felt a sharp pain on her head and everything going black, she realized she should've paid better attention.

Chapter Fifteen

Marion Drumsky arrived at Midlands Hospital, a hood pulled over her head. She avoided as many people as possible, ducking into doorways or turning her back to them as she made her way through the halls to the third floor. She used the stairs instead of the elevator before she made her way to Sam Meyers' room. She didn't want a million people knowing she was there.

She located the room and entered swiftly, shutting the door behind her. Marion leaned with her back against it as she took a moment to push the top of her hoodie back while watching the drips of the IV and listening to the monitors Sam was hooked up to as they made monotonous beeps.

Slowly, Marion moved across the room so as not to disturb Sam enough to wake him. Sam didn't move and Marion almost breathed a sigh of relief when she arrived between the bed and the monitors. Reaching in her pocket, she pulled out a round object, rubbing the piece gently with her thumb. She took a step forward, her eyes unreadable.

She was good with her potions. That was her gift and her strength for the coven, but her powers, her gifts, were never supposed to be used for personal gain. As she stared down at the unconscious man, she couldn't help reaching over to place her hand on his, her features softening as they touched. Not only would her coven be upset, but her husband would be furious if he knew she was here, much less what she planned on doing.

Pulling her hand back, she pushed his teeth apart to open them up slightly before she moved the small object over his lips and cracked it. The effervescent liquid dripped into the small aperture of his mouth, making its way down his throat and into his system. She planned on staying with him to see the effect her potion would have, but knew she could be caught if she did so.

Marion jumped when she heard the bathroom toilet flush, then water running. She ran past the closed bathroom door and entered the hallways, pulling her hoodie up to hide her features from the people she passed and the cameras. She barely escaped just as the on-duty officer emerged from using the facilities.

Officer James Lumely looked towards the closed door of the room, then back at the sleeping man on the bed. He could've sworn he heard something, but nothing appeared disturbed. Still, he pulled the door open and glanced down the corridors, looking first one way and then the next. Nothing. Closing the door, he sat down and stared at the monitors before pulling out a gun magazine. He gave a final look at the monitors, then settled in to read.

Chapter Sixteen

Gumshoe had the distinct feeling something was wrong. He noticed Mia had put on her enchanted necklace that morning, enabling them to speak to each other without the actual use of vocalizations. Although he wasn't sure how far the necklace would work, or if they had to have line of sight, he thought he'd try it out anyways. *"Mia? Can you hear me, baby doll?"*

When he didn't get any answer, he trotted over to the corner and peeked around. His rich, blue eyes widened. A car sped away and he recognized it as the one he saw yesterday morning at the Hennessys' house. Worse, Mia was nowhere to be seen and the sign she'd made and carried laid discarded haphazardly on the ground by her bike. This time he could see the car better. He had to get help.

Running back towards her group of friends, he noticed Detective Hardy standing on the perimeter, along with several other officers. They were probably there to ensure the safety of those in the march. He didn't waste any time as he ran to the Detective, jumped on a tree nearby, then launched onto Phil's head. Leaning forward, he put his mouth next to Phil's ear and meowed as loudly as he could.

Phil about jumped three feet into the air as he was suddenly attacked by the Siamese he hadn't even seen coming. He wasn't even sure what was going on or what was on his head. He yelled for someone to get it off him as he waved his arms, flailing about, trying to capture the creature.

The officers were laughing, but Easton reached over and grabbed the cat, setting him down on the ground. "Guess he doesn't like you much." He chuckled.

Once free of the feline, Phil rubbed his head and looked down. The cat was still mewing loudly and turning in circles. "Wait. That's Mia's new cat." Lifting his head, he looked around for the girl before returning his gaze to the Siamese. "Where is Mia? Is something wrong?"

"It's not a dog, detective." Easton laughed harder.

"Maybe not, but he might be intelligent enough to know she's in trouble or something."

Gumshoe stopped turning around in circles, nodded his head and started to head back to where the bikes were parked. Phil followed him. If it was a wild goose chase, at least he knew he tried. On the other hand, if something was really wrong, having never seen a cat act like this before, he'd pay more attention in the future to what this cat had to say.

Knowing he was being followed, Gumshoe ran faster and stopped by the fallen sign, giving Phil a very plaintive meow. Phil reached the sign, picked it up, and noticed Mia's bike wasn't quite locked up, a good indication she'd been interrupted before doing so. Phil pulled out his walkie talkie. "Get a BOLO alert on Mia Thomas, stat." He looked down at the cat. "I wish you could talk and let me know what happened."

Gumshoe looked around, then moved to Mia's sign. He sat in front of it, then mewed to get Phil's attention as he put one paw in the air waving it slightly, his body tilted on the side. Phil looked at the sign, the words jumping out at him. *Fear has no place in our Schools. Protect Kids not guns. #Enough!*

Phil was astonished. This was the freakiest thing he'd ever seen. He dropped the sign on the ground and turned, but Gumshoe mewed loudly to get his attention once again. He then put his paw on the C in schools. A cat who could spell? Who was trying to communicate with him in an intelligent way? Yet, something told him to trust the cat enough to see what he'd spell out, despite how crazy it seemed. It might end up not even a real word, or might say he wants tuna. Phil pulled out his notepad, jotting down each letter. C-A-R. Car. F-O-R-D. Ford. G-D. What was that? Then he noticed Gumshoe tapping his paw three times. "Three?" The feline nodded. Then tapped again. "Five?" Gumshoe nodded and repeated the process until he was done. "GD 3513. What is this supposed to mean? Wait? Is this a plate?" The cat nodded.

"Well, holy crap. This is amazing. You're the most talented feline I've ever heard of." He pulled the walkie talkie out and gave a quick description of the vehicle they were looking for, as well as the license plate. When he finished, he looked at the cat. "You're either a freaking amazing furball or pulling my chain and wasting my time, but I'm not taking the chance you're not right. You better stay by me until we find her."

"Mew." Gumshoe agreed and pranced over to him.

Phil bent down and gathered the sign again. "By the way, this is between the two of us. Otherwise, they might strip me of my badge and throw me in the loony bin."

Chapter Seventeen

Mia came to with a throbbing headache. She wasn't exactly sure where she was, but it was dark, smelled bad, and felt like a bumpy ride. In the trunk of a stinky car. She held onto her necklace and tried to reach out to Gumshoe. *"Gumshoe? Can you hear me?"*

"Yes. I've been so worried about you. Where are you?"

"I'm not sure. In the trunk of a car. It's moving, but I can't see anything."

"Do you know who's driving? Did you see him?"

"No. He surprised me and hit me over the head. I must've blacked out. I just woke up a couple of minutes ago."

"I felt something off and got that flatfoot friend of yours. It took some convincing, and I don't think he's totally sure of me yet, but he's looking for the car. This time I got the plate."

"How did you convey the information? Are you talking to him now, too?"

"Not in the way you mean. I used your sign for letters and paw taps for numbers. He isn't quite sure he believes me yet and thinks it's pretty much some science

fiction thing going on, but he did put the word out to look for the car and you."

"If only I could see, I could tell you where I was." Mia sighed. She wished she could pop open the trunk. Assuming nothing would happen, but feeling like trying anyways, she flipped her wrist. "Open." Color her surprised when the trunk actually obeyed. She quickly grabbed the top so it wouldn't open completely, informing the driver of its release. However, she opened it enough to peer outside. *"Gumshoe, I did it. I opened the trunk and can see out."*

"Great. You found your power. Tell me what you see."

"Nothing but land at the moment. Wait. I think I see a sign. It's the back. Hopefully there will be one facing me. Yes. There it is. Crap. We're on Highway 31. I think we're headed back to Mr. Meyers' encampment. Do you think he's going to kill me there?"

"Not if I can help it."

Mia wasn't sure what, if anything, he was going to be able to do, but regardless, she trusted him. The vehicle turned onto a dirt road, making her bounce all over the place and barely hold onto the trunk lid. When the vehicle finally came to a stop, she lifted the trunk wide enough to roll out, then quietly closed it before running to hide behind the bushes. She barely made it before she saw him get out of the driver's seat and head towards the rear of the green Ford Escort, the blade of a shiny knife glinting in the sun.

Chapter Eighteen

"Come on, Mia. It'll be quick, I promise." Earl Dapper looked under the car and then around the nearby bushes, knowing she wasn't too far when he realized she wasn't in the trunk. Had she jumped out while the car was still moving, the trunk would've been wide open and he would've noticed immediately. Plus, she would've been hurt had she tried to jump out of a moving vehicle. Logically, Earl surmised, she had to be somewhere near.

Mia wanted to answer. Wanted to find out why Earl did all this. What did he have to gain by destroying the restaurant's reputation and her dad's in the process? Why kill the Hennessys? Why kill Henry and try to kill Mr. Meyers? What did they all have in common? And now, she was on his list, but even that generated a why? Suddenly, stupidly, she felt like Maddie asking a dozen why questions with no real answers that made any sense to her and wishing Maddie's gold rope really worked in getting the truth.

He came perilously close. She held her breath, afraid to move, lest he discover her. Earl kept talking. "I like your dad. Adam is a great chef and a great guy."

"Then, why?" It slipped out before she could stop herself, and she covered her mouth, holding her breath.

Earl spun around and carefully started towards the area he heard her. If he could get her to talk again, she might give her location away and he'd have her. "He's too good. I knew business was going to drop because of him. People came to my place because of him, not his sous Jeremy, who's nothing but an accident waiting to happen. Ruining your dad's business means he'd need another job and he'd come crawling back to me for it."

When he passed her hiding place, she moved as quietly as she could to another location farther away, cautiously avoiding the leaves and other brush that'd signal her progress. "Why me?" she whispered as she moved, then stopped and held her breath, lest he find her from her question.

He paused, listening towards where he heard her voice. It had come on the wind and he wasn't sure in which direction it originated. Guessing, he started his hunt again. "I couldn't take the chance of you saying you saw me at the hospital. I wasn't expecting a cop stationed there."

"Baby doll? What's going on? Are you still okay?" Gumshoe rang inside her head and she almost jumped

with his intrusion, stepping on a twig and hearing it snap under her foot. A sheen of sweat broke out on her forehead with her fear of being caught by Earl.

She'd totally forgotten her new companion and the ability her necklace had given her to speak to him long distances. *"I'm at the woods entrance of where we found Mr. Meyers. It's Earl. He's trying to kill me now."*

"I'll figure out something to get the flatfoot to you a.s.a.p. Just hang in there."

She found a boulder next to a bush, and huddled there, trying to breathe shallowly so as not to be found.

Earl stopped and turned back around when he heard the snap of wood continuing to listen for any sound of movement, or hoping she'd ask another question to indicate where she might be.

She wanted to know more, and then wondered if she could make a sound farther away immediately after she asked it, like she did when she popped the trunk. Or was the trunk a fluke? Looking around, she noticed a small branch hanging precariously. Concentrating, Mia tried to get the branch to brake. Nothing happened. How had she performed the small miracle of the trunk before? She was scared. She was desperate. She focused her energies, just as Mrs. Antonio told her in the private lesson on the night of her birthday, despite anything actually happening.

"Focus is key to everything. Feel the earth beneath your feet, the wind in your hair, the sun on your face. This is what you are tied to, Mia. This is where you will draw your energies. When you are one with the world around you, you'll be able to accomplish great things." Mrs. Antonio's voice rang in her head, as if she were actually there.

Breathing slowly, Mia closed her eyes to the branch, imagining it only in her head as she saw it moments ago. "Break." She heard a crack and opened her eyes in time to see the limb splinter and fall to the ground. It wasn't easy, but she'd done it. She couldn't help but smile. She'd done it!

Earl couldn't miss the sound and headed quickly toward the broken branch, then looked around for her, almost frantically.

Keep him talking until Phil comes. Before she would verbally speak, she looked around again for something that would immediately distract him from her actual location. "And the Hennessys? They were a sweet, old couple." Using her newfound powers, she made a small pile of stones tumble away from her towards where Mr. Meyers' camp had been situated.

Earl spun around again and started towards the path. "They were my cousins. They owned the land where I'm sure you discovered the truffles. I wanted the land; they wouldn't sell, but told me they would will it to me. I just helped them along to their eternal rest. I just can't find the damned deed. Do you know where it is?"

Mia figured he must've realized her deception as he turned right towards her instead of entering the woods farther. Her heart beat faster. Was he hearing it? Or her rapid, shallow breathing, then small gasps of breath just to get air into her lungs? He was close, and Mia became even more fearful, especially when the sun glinted off the knife once again. She could barely think, much less focus. Her eyes scanned everything she could think of, then went back to the branch. "Move," she commanded softly, trying to remember everything she was taught in the process. The branch raised itself from the ground, hovering slightly about waist high, then flew across the air towards Earl.

Earl sensed the shift in the air, but turned only in time to see a disembodied piece of wood fling itself at his head to splinter and crack under the force of the weight. Both dropped like a stone to the ground.

Mia didn't waste any time and ran with everything she had towards the car and then the road. She noticed a car headed her way and she waved her arms over her head, frantically crying for help. The car stopped near her, the door being flung open. Gumshoe hopped onto the ground just as a pant-suited leg slipped past the door. Phil stood, grabbing her as he asked if she was okay. As she nodded, he asked where her assailant was and she pointed back towards the trail. "It's Earl," she whispered, slightly out of breath.

Phil nodded. "Stay with the car. Others are right behind me. Afterwards, you and I are going to have a serious discussion about your insanely crazy cat." He pulled the gun from his holster and headed cautiously towards Earl's car and the woods just beyond. "Earl? You're surrounded. Come out with your hands up. There's no running now."

When there was absolutely no sound and backup had arrived, Phil continued quickly, finding the unconscious body of Earl. He had one of the units call for an ambulance and asked Officer Figoe to remain until help arrived.

Gumshoe purred around Mia's legs, then followed as Officer Easton brought her to the ambulance that just arrived. A second ambulance appeared and their crew headed into the woods to get Earl. Sitting on the ground, Gumshoe lifted a leg and started to lick on the inside of his thigh, his paw standing straight out.

While the EMTs took care of Earl, Phil walked back to Mia. He dismissed Kevin and waited until the medics indicated she was okay to talk with.

Chapter Nineteen

"You have the strangest and smartest cat I've ever encountered. For only having him for a couple of days, he sure has become attached to you. It's because of him we realized you were even missing, and then how to find you. This...amazing cat can even spell. I've never seen anything like it."

"He's very special, Phil. He and I developed a strong connection our first day together." Mia shifted uncomfortably. She'd been warned not to tell others she was a witch, or that her new feline companion was a reincarnated private detective from who knows how long ago. However, Gumshoe showing off, even to save her life, left her discombobulated in how to respond. "I'm glad he was able to guide you to where I was. I don't know how long it would've been before Earl found me."

"What's your cat's name again?"

"Gumshoe."

"How appropriate." He chuckled slightly. "He was quite insistent about getting my attention. I've got the scratches to prove it."

"I'm very sorry he hurt you."

Phil shrugged. "I'll take a million more if it means

keeping you safe."

That was the kind of relationship Phil and Mia had. He treated her like a beloved niece and she thought of him as a kind uncle. She leaned against his arm. "Will Dad be free now?"

"I've already told the sheriff to let him go." He wrapped his arm around her. "He should be home by now." He looked up and smiled. "Or not." Phil nodded to something behind Mia.

She turned her head and squealed in happiness, jumping off the back of the ambulance and running to her parents. Although she was thrilled to see her mother, it was her father who she almost tackled.

"Whoa!" Adam laughed, hugging his daughter tightly. "Thank you." He kissed her temple before letting her go. "I appreciate all you did to help free me. I'm also upset you got so involved you were almost killed, but we'll talk about that later. Right now, I'm just glad you're alright."

Mia blushed at his praise, her cheeks getting a deeper red when he chastised her, albeit lightly. She knew she should've stayed out of police business, but if she had, she wouldn't have found out who the culprit was, and Earl might've succeeded in getting away with his plans. Sadly, those plans included the destruction of her family's business and reputation.

Phil appeared next to her and stuck his hand out to Adam. "I hope we're still good, man."

Adam nodded and shook his hand. "I know you were just doing your job. I also know you worked very hard in getting me free as soon as possible. It's all good."

"I'll see you all later. I'm going to try and interview Earl and see what this was all about." Phil was about to leave when Mia stopped him.

"Ask him about the deed to the Hennessys' property out here. He told me it was why he killed them. The property was supposed to be left to him by the Hennessys, as he's their cousin, and I guess they told him they would give it to him when they died, and he helped them along."

"What is so important about this land?"

"It holds truffles."

Phil gave her a 'so what' kind of look. Adam pat Phil on the shoulder. "Truffles are one of the most expensive ingredients around, depending on the type."

"Dad, these are black diamond."

Adam paled. "Holy shit."

Again, Phil looked between them. "Explain?"

"Black diamonds are *the* most expensive truffles out there. They can go for $1,000 a pound, just to start, and it's not unheard of to be even more costly. A shaving alone can cost you close to $100." Adam ran his hand through his hair. "You mean to tell me this is all over land where black diamonds are growing? We have them here?"

Mia nodded. "Gumshoe found them when we were looking for Mr. Meyers. I didn't know what they were at first until I talked to Mr. Meyers in the hospital."

"It would stand to reason, Samuel told Earl about the truffles. I know Sam is rather close to Earl. And if that's the case, it'd explain why Earl tried to off Sam." Phil shifted from one foot to the other as he mentally started to put the puzzle together.

"Which would make Earl greedy enough to try and get them for his own restaurant. Depending on how many there are around here, and how carefully they're harvested, he could've had a billion dollar fortune. But, why go after me? I wouldn't care if he found a trove of truffles." Adam wrapped his arm around Mia, taking Eve's hand with the other.

"Because he wanted you to come back to his

restaurant as head chef. He thought if he put you out of business and ruined your reputation, you'd come crawling back for your old job."

Phil frowned. "Why go after you?"

"I wondered that myself." Mia wrapped her arms around her father's waist, feeling safe. "I can only assume he thought I knew more than I did and was afraid I'd spill the beans on him being behind all of this."

"One thing we also don't know is why he killed Henry." Phil pulled out his notepad and made a couple of notes.

"Because he was a loose end. Most likely he hired Henry to poison the soup, and thereby the Hennessys. From the conversation we heard in the alleyway, Henry couldn't be trusted enough to remain silent." Gumshoe sat by Mia, curling his tail around his front legs, the tip twitching.

Mia got the message and relayed it to the detective. Phil's eyebrows raised in surprise. "I should hire you and Gumshoe to be part of my detective team."

"Not at this time. She's a chef." Adam pulled her closer.

Mia nodded. She was definitely a chef first, but she

had to admit, it was fun trying to find who was the murderer. Even if she almost died in the process. Only thing was, now she had a weapon no one would expect: the power of telekinesis. And she was going to perfect it.

Chapter Twenty

A week had gone by since Earl was discovered to be the mastermind behind the whole mushroom poisoning affair, as well as being responsible for the deaths of Henry, Katie, and the Hennessys. Thankfully, no one else had the amount of poison as the latter three, and therefore were well on their way to a full recovery. Only Samuel Meyers had been uncertain at first, thought by many of the hospital staff to be joining the ranks of those deceased. It was later discovered Sam had been given a potent shot directly into his blood stream. It should've killed him directly, but he somehow managed to survive for the hospital to treat him. Even so, they were sure his heart would give out, as well as his other organs. They even had him on a waitlist for transplants. Somehow, he fully recovered. Mia had visited him twice over the past few days.

He was able to fill her in on a couple of details Phil and the others weren't quite ready to share with the general public, but Sam felt since she saved his life, he owed her some explanations. "I hadn't realized when I told Earl about finding such a gold mine that he'd go to such lengths as to kill people. I told him it was private land, but I found the truffles by accident, not realizing I'd wandered onto private property. He told me not to say anything and he'd find the land owners and offer to buy it. If they didn't know what was there, they'd be more willing to sell it. If only I'd known." Sam wailed.

Mia shook her head as she sat next to the monitors Sam was still hooked up to. "How could anyone know? You've known Earl for decades. Sadly, no one really understands what makes a person tick. Dad tells me that often."

"Your father is a smart man, Mia. I'd never have done anything on purpose to put him or his family in danger. I thought Earl was going to find who owned the land and make him an offer for it. When I realized what he'd done, I told him I was going to go to the police and confess my part in it, but I wouldn't implicate him. Guess he didn't believe me."

"Or he didn't want to take the chance. As greedy as he was, it's hard to trust others. I know he considered Henry a loose end after he paid him to use the poisonous mushrooms. How did he poison you? Did you eat them?"

Sam shook his head. "No. I'd been hiding out where you found me from the police. I didn't know what to do, so I thought it best to keep to myself where no one could find me until I figured things out. Earl suspected I might go there to stay low. When I told him I was going to turn myself in, he seemed to take it calmly, but then I turned my back on him. Worse thing ever. Next thing I knew, I felt a pinch against my arm and everything suddenly wavered before my eyes. Next thing I knew, you were there telling me to hold on as you were going to get help. The cops found a discarded syringe in the bushes by my tent and the doctors figured out the reason I got so bad so quickly was 'cause the poison was injected into my blood stream directly. Seems he had some of the mushrooms left over and dried them up, ground them down, and mixed them with something to make them fluid. Probably just water, but who knows?"

"I'm glad they were able to figure out how to save you, considering."

"That's the thing. It's more of a miracle. They didn't think their treatment was working, and in all honesty, it shouldn't have. But somehow, it did. They're going to release me tomorrow. The docs want to poke me for as long as they can, but honestly, I don't care. I still feel a bit weak to be on my own."

Mia knew Sam didn't have much in the way of

family to care for him. He lived by himself, without even a pet to keep him company. He seemed okay with it, until now. It was always nice to go home and know someone would be there if one needed help while recovering, or just to keep one company. "If you'd like, I can try and stop by between school and work. We are reopening the restaurant again. Now that word got out how Earl was behind it all, people are making reservations again, anxious to come back."

"I'm so glad. Your dad is a great chef, and from what I've heard, you're going to be just as great, if not more so."

Mia felt her cheeks heat up and knew she was blushing. She lowered her eyes demurely. "I'm just glad we're getting back up and running again. It was only a couple of weeks, but it seemed like forever."

"I'd love for you to visit any time you wish."

As Mia stood to leave, she was surprised when the door opened and Mrs. Drumsky walked in. They both stopped, staring at each other, before Marion moved to indicate she'd like a private word with Mia in the hallway and out of ear shot of Sam.

Obliging her, Mia said another good-bye to Sam and waited in the hallway for Marion to join her. "Mrs.

Drumsky. I didn't know you were close to Mr. Meyers."

Marion looked around nervously before she gave Mia a piercing stare. "Many don't know this, but Sam, Mr. Meyers, is my half-brother, and I've come to offer him my home while he is still convalescing."

"I'm glad. He shouldn't be alone just yet. Why the secrecy?"

"Because of what I did to heal him. Oh, you mean why don't others know we're related?"

"Yes, but now I'm curious what you did to cure him. Wait. You used a spell or potion or something. You told me we aren't supposed to use magic for personal gain." Mia harshly whispered, her mind racing.

"You're not. However, I'm willing to take the consequences, though, in order to protect my only sibling, even if he is only half. We shared the same father, so we weren't raised together, but we've grown close over the past few years when we found out we shared a father, which we discovered at our dad's funeral. It was a huge surprise and I'm just not ready to let him die needlessly. Please. Don't tell your mother or the others in the coven." She almost begged for understanding.

Mia gave it some thought, but then nodded. "I

won't tell anyone. Not even Mom. If I could've saved him myself, I would've. I don't blame you on not wanting to lose anyone else to something so inane as poison mushrooms. There's been enough death as it is. My lips are sealed."

Marion reached over and gave Mia a hug. "Thank you." Pulling back, she headed into the room to visit Sam.

Mia paused in the hallway for a few minutes, smiling. Her mom hadn't let her do what she wanted in saving Mr. Meyers or the others who were sick, but Mrs. Drumsky did, and Mia would keep her word by not telling another soul.

Although, as it turned out, she didn't have to. Mrs. Antonio, Miss Lucas and her mom all knew, because once Mr. Meyers miraculously recovered, Mrs. Drumsky refused to leave her home. Her mother didn't want Mia to know what price Mrs. Drumsky paid, but Mrs. Antonio felt Mia needed to get an idea what consequences are paid when one used their powers for personal reasons or in changing the normal course of the universe, like preventing someone's death.

Donna took Mia to Marion's home, so she could observe for herself one of a multitude of consequences.

At first Marion didn't want to let either of them in, but she knew Donna was relentless when she set her mind to it. Marion wasn't about to continue arguing when she knew it was a lost cause. Mrs. Antonio tended to be very stubborn when she had a point to make or a lesson to teach.

"We won't stay long, Marion. Just open the door long enough for Mia to see what price you are paying for saving Samuel."

The door clicked, then parted slightly. Donna gave Mia a slight push to enter the darkened foyer. Looking behind her, Mia realized Mrs. Antonio wasn't going to accompany her. Taking a breath to steady her nerves, Mia moved farther into the home. The drapes were drawn, the house cast in a dark gloom. "Mrs. Drumsky?"

"In here, child."

Mia headed towards the voice, but stopped when she saw her sitting on the couch. "I'm sorry we disturbed you."

"I understand why Donna brought you here. It's to give you an understanding of the consequences we talked about. Turn on the light, so you can see what my payment is."

Mia looked around for the light switch before

flicking it on. She gasped in shock when she saw Marion covered in scales from head to toe, looking a bit reptilian. "Will it? Are you going to stay like that forever?"

"No. It'll last for a few weeks, then disappear and I'll be back to normal."

"Is it always the same punishment?"

"No. It varies on the witch and the spell. Each consequence is as individual as the situation. For me, I cheated death for Sam. Snakes are a symbol for a life force and for rebirth. It's only fitting that I be forced to bear the scales for my deed. Please turn the light back out."

Mia reached for the switch, casting the room once again in darkness. She didn't know what more to say. The woman barely looked human, and she had to admit she was badly shaken over Marion's punishment. Mia stayed only moments more before she headed back out to Mrs. Antonio, but she had to admit she'd give great thought before she ever broke the rule of using magic for personal gain.

With the restaurant reopened, things were finally starting to get back to normal. Mia breathed a sigh of relief. The deed, which was so important to Earl, was found in the barn with the cow. It was such a surprise to find it in such a strange location, but it was even more of a surprise to Phil that Gumshoe was the one who led them there, and he was still astounded by what the cat could do. He even wanted to film him and put him on TV. "We'll be rich," he exclaimed. "With the money he could make you, Mia, you could go to any top-five school you wanted and not worry how to pay for it." Mia knew Phil was referring to Harvard, Yale, Princeton, Stanford and MIT.

"I'm good, Phil. My cat is special, granted, but he ain't gonna be exploited. Sorry."

"Was just thinking of you, Mia." Phil patted her on her head, which he knew she hated. It was his way of teasing her.

Chapter Twenty-One

Mia closed the bedroom door and pulled out her computer. She had a name, and though she didn't have a date, she might be able to find something regardless. She waited until the computer warmed up, then entered Alexander Owens, Private Eye into the search engine.

Gumshoe remembered his last name earlier in the day, when there was a delivery truck with the name Owen Johnson and Sons Delivery. The name jogged Gumshoe's memory and he knew Alexander was his first name and Owens was the last. He followed Mia around the rest of the day, anxious for her to sit and look on the magic machine for any clue to his past human life. After an eternity of waiting for the day to wind down, they were finally home and able to start looking into his background. Gumshoe fidgeted, walking back and forth as he waited for Mia to do the legwork of locating any information for him. Finally, he jumped on the bed behind her. Gumshoe peered over her shoulder, hoping something, anything would appear familiar. His tail flicked back and forth in his nervous agitation.

Mia knew how important this was for him. She had to find something to help him fill in those memory gaps.

He barely remembered his own name. There were many Alexander Owens the search engine revealed, but only a couple of private eyes. Mia was able to narrow it down to three that looked promising. Pulling up the first one, who was born in 1852 and died in 1923, she pulled back and let Gumshoe look to see if the man in the photograph of his obituary sparked any memories. After a moment, Gumshoe shook his head.

"It's okay. There are two more we can check, and if they don't turn up anything, I'll do something else to find you. There has got to be a record of your life somewhere."

She pulled up the second Alexander profile. This one was born 1901 and died 1944 while serving in World War II.

Gumshoe pressed his nose closer. *"I remember the war. I think I was in it."*

"That's great. Do you think this is the one?"

Gumshoe took longer to look at the man in uniform. It was a bit fuzzy, but he ended up shaking his head after an extended period of time examining the picture. *"No."*

"They say three's the charm," Mia encouraged him and pulled up the third profile.

Alexander Owens. Born 1917. Served in World

War II. Honorably discharged. Murdered in 1947, leaving behind a wife, Elizabeth, and a young daughter, Martha. Murderer was never caught.

Gumshoe read and reread the short obituary, his blue eyes watering up. *"I remember. Elizabeth was my wife. She'd just given birth to my daughter. Martha was my mother's name. That's me."*

Mia frowned, looking back at the computer. "Says you were murdered, and the killer was never discovered. I think we have a new case."

Gumshoe, despite being a feline, gave her the look of total appreciation. *"Thank you. I'd like to know all of that. What happened to my family? Are any of them still alive? And why was I killed?"*

"I promise, Gumshoe. We're going to find what happened to you and your family."

Mia's Opening Night Dinner Menu

Five Mushroom Soup:

The secret to this deep, rich soup is a long slow caramelization.

Ingredients

- 1/4 cup unsalted butter
- 2 pounds sliced fresh mushrooms: Use a mix of crimini, oyster, shitake, porteenies (small portello) and chanterelle's
- 1 pinch salt
- 1 yellow onion, diced
- 1 1/2 tablespoons all-purpose flour
- 6 sprigs fresh thyme
- 2 cloves garlic, peeled and finely chopped
- 4 cups chicken broth
- 1 cup water
- 1 cup heavy whipping cream
- 1 pinch salt and ground black pepper to taste
- 1 teaspoon fresh thyme leaves for garnish.

Directions

1. Melt butter in a large soup pot over medium-high heat; cook mushrooms in butter with 1 pinch salt until the mushrooms give off their juices; reduce heat to low. Continue to cook, stirring often, until juices evaporate and the mushrooms are golden brown, about 15 minutes. Set aside a few attractive mushroom slices for garnish later, if desired. Mix onion into

mushrooms and cook until onion is soft and translucent, about 5 more minutes.

2. Stir flour into mushroom mixture and cook, stirring often, for 2 minutes to remove raw flour taste. Tie thyme sprigs into a small bundle with kitchen twine and add to mushroom mixture; add garlic cloves. Pour chicken stock and water into mushroom mixture. Bring to a simmer and cook for 1 hour. Remove thyme bundle.

3. Transfer soup to a blender in small batches and puree on high speed until smooth and thick.

4. Return soup to pot and stir in cream. Season with salt and black pepper and serve in bowls, garnished with reserved mushroom slices and a few thyme leaves.

Pear and Arugula Salad with Cranberry Orange Dressing

Ingredients for the Salad

- 5 cups green lettuce, romaine or baby spinach chopped
- 5 cups arugula
- 2 pears, cored and sliced
- 1/2 cup dried cranberries (optional)

For the Oat Pecan Clusters
- 1 and 1/2 cup chopped pecans
- 1/2 cup rolled oats
- 3 tablespoons raw honey (or brown rice syrup)
- 2 tablespoons coconut sugar
- 1/4 teaspoon salt

Cranberry Orange Dressing
- 12 ounces cranberries, fresh or frozen
- 1/3 cup raw honey (or maple syrup/brown rice syrup)
- 1/3 cup apple cider vinegar 1 cup orange juice
- 2 tablespoons orange zest (from two oranges)
- 1 tablespoons Dijon mustard pinch salt & pepper

Directions
1. To make the dressing, combine the cranberries with the honey, apple cider vinegar and orange juice in a small pot over medium heat. Bring to a boil and cook for about 10 minutes, or until the cranberries are soft enough to break open. Remove from the heat and set aside to cool. Once the cranberries have cooled, add them to a blender with the orange zest, mustard and salt & pepper. Blend on high until smooth then transfer to a sealed

container.

2. To make the pecan oat clusters, preheat the oven to 300°F and then line a baking sheet with parchment paper. Combine the pecans, oats, coconut sugar and salt in a small bowl and stir together. Drizzle the honey (or brown rice syrup) on top and stir until all of the pecans are well coated and begin to stick together with the oats. Transfer the mixture to the baking sheet and use your hands to press it down in a large circle, making sure that it's one large piece that holds together. Bake in the oven for 18 minutes then set aside to cool completely before breaking into pieces.

3. Assemble the salad by combining greens of choice with the arugula and the pear in a large bowl. Add the pecan oat clusters and the dried cranberries and toss together. Serve with the cranberry orange dressing on the side and enjoy!

Notes Store leftover dressing in airtight container in the refrigerator for up to one week.

Duck Breasts with Red Wine and Orange Sauce

Ingredients

- 4 duck breasts, well-trimmed
- 2 shallots, finely chopped
- 300mls red wine - approx. 2 glasses
- Zest of 1 orange
- Juice of 2 oranges
- Salt and black pepper
- 2 teaspoon Red currant jelly
- 1 teaspoon Corn flour mixed with 1 tablespoon
- water

Directions

1. Heat a large pan. Score the skin on the duck breasts and place them in the hot pan, skin side down. You don't need any oil in the pan. Brown well then remove to a plate.
2. Pour off most of the fat - leave about 1 tablespoon in the pan. Add in the shallots and cook for about five minutes to soften.
3. Add in the red wine, orange zest, orange juice and seasoning and bring to the boil.
4. Place the duck breasts back in the pan and simmer for ten minutes.
5. Remove the duck from the pan and cover with foil to keep warm while you finish the sauce.
6. Add the red currant jelly and corn flour mixture into the pan and bring to the boil, stirring all the time.
7. Reduce to simmer for a couple of minutes.
8. Slice the duck breasts and place on serving plates. Spoon the sauce around the duck and serve.

Oven Roasted Brussels Sprouts with Bacon

Ingredients

- 1½ pounds Brussels sprouts
- 2 tablespoons olive oil
- Kosher salt and freshly ground black pepper
- 6 bacon slices, cut into 1 inch pieces

Directions

1. Preheat oven to 400 degrees.
2. Clean and trim Brussels sprouts and cutting any very large heads in half through the core. (It's fine if some of the outer leaves fall off – just bake those along with the rest of the sprouts. They get extra crispy and are delicious!)
3. Place the Brussels sprouts in a large bowl and drizzle with olive oil, tossing to evenly coat.
4. Pour the Brussels sprouts onto a large sheet pan (you want them to be in a single layer).
5. Sprinkle with salt and pepper.
6. Then evenly sprinkle the bacon pieces over the Brussels sprouts.
7. Roast in the oven for 20 to 30 minutes, turning halfway through the cooking time, until golden and lightly caramelized.
8. Serve immediately.

Twice-Baked Sweet Potatoes

Ingredients

- 4 Medium sweet potatoes (About 10 ounces each)
- 4 ounces cream cheese, softened.
- 2 tablespoons brown sugar
- ½ teaspoon ground cinnamon
- 4 tablespoons chopped pecans

Directions

1. Preheat oven to 375 degrees. Scrub potatoes. pierce several times with a fork. Bake on a foil – lined baking sheet until tender, 45-60 minutes. Cool slightly.
2. Cut off a thin slice from top of each potato. Scoop out pulp, leaving ¼ inch thick shells. Mash pulp with cream cheese, brown sugar and cinnamon.
3. Spoon into shells, return to pan. Top with pecans. Baked until heated through. 15-20 minutes.

Easy Chocolate Crème Brule

Ingredients

- 1 quart heavy cream
- 1/2 cup white sugar
- 2 teaspoons vanilla extract
- 9 egg yolks
- 1/2 cup chocolate chips
- 2 tablespoons white sugar, or as needed

Directions

1. Preheat oven to 325 degrees F (165 degrees C). Set 6 (6 ounce) ramekins on a baking sheet.
2. Pour cream, sugar, and vanilla into a saucepan, and place over medium heat. Stir to dissolve the sugar, and heat until it begins to simmer, then remove from heat. Place egg yolks in a large bowl, and slowly whisk in the hot cream mixture, about 2 tablespoons at a time, until you have added approximately a cup of cream to the yolks. At this point, pour in the remaining cream, and whisk until smooth. Stir in the chocolate chips, and set aside for 5 minutes.
3. Stir the mixture until the chocolate is smooth and evenly distributed. Pour into ramekins, and bake in preheated oven until the center is just set, 15 to 20 minutes. Remove from oven, and allow to cool for 45 minutes, then place into the refrigerator, and chill until cold, about 6 hours.
4. Place oven rack in topmost position. Turn oven to broil.
5. Sprinkle the tops of each crème Brule with sugar until evenly coated, gently pour off excess sugar.

Place ramekins onto a baking sheet, and place under the broiler until the sugar bubbles and turns a light caramel brown. Serve immediately.

ABOUT THE AUTHOR

Ms. Hawks has always been interested in writing in some form or other, including writing for a local newspaper. Deciding to become more knowledgeable, she headed back to school and received her Master's Degree in Ancient Civilizations, Native American History and United States History.

It was at this time she got involved in role playing on FaceBook, which gave her ample opportunities to grow and hone her writing ability.

She lives in the suburbs of Chicago with her four companions, all males... cats. She travels as much as she can to various Author/Reader conventions and loves to meet established fans and make new ones, some of which she considers friends more than fans. Check out her social media sites to follow her.

WebSite: AuthorLauraHawks.com
Twitter: AuthorLHawks
FB Author page:
https://www.facebook.com/LauraHawks-249262585192270/?fref=ts
FB Fan Group: Hawks Flock:
https://www.facebook.com/groups

Made in the USA
Monee, IL
15 March 2022